14

# TALES of TIKKUN

# TALES *of* TIKKUN

## New Jewish Stories to Heal the Wounded World

Phyllis Ocean Berman and
Arthur Ocean Waskow

JASON ARONSON INC.
*Northvale, New Jersey*
*London*

This book was set in 11 pt. Goudy OldStyle by FASTpages of Nanuet, NY.

Library of Congress Cataloging-in-Publication Data

Berman, Phyllis Ocean, 1942–
    Tales of Tikkun : new Jewish stories to heal the wounded world /
Phyllis Ocean Berman, Arthur Ocean Waskow
        p.   cm.
    ISBN 1–56821–991–1 (alk. paper)
    1. Legends, Jewish.   2. Midrash.   3. Bible.   O.T.—Legends.
I. Waskow, Arthur Ocean, 1933–      .   II. Title.
BM530.B496   1996
296.1'9—dc20                                                96–32547
                                                                CIP

Manufactured in the United States of America. Jason Aronson Inc. offers books and cassettes. For information and catalog write to Jason Aronson Inc., 230 Livingston Street, Northvale, New Jersey 07647.

Once in every generation there arises a rebbe who does not seek to create mere followers — hassidim — but seeks instead to light the spark of rebbehood in everyone.

Once in every generation there arises a teacher who learns from every other teacher — and from every student.

Once in every generation there arises a lover-and-beloved who radiates a love so deep that in all the souls it touches it awakens a deeper willingness to love.

Once in every generation there arises a dancer who embodies in music and mime, in every storyteller's shrug and gesture, that every bone shall praise You.

And once in every era there arises someone who unites all four of these.

For our rebbe,
our teacher, our student,
our graceful partner in the circle-dance,
our friend:
Zalman Schachter-Shalomi.

# Table of Contents

## Table of Contents

# Twice Upon a Time:
# An Introduction

"*Tikkun*" means the healing of what is wounded, the mending of what is shattered. In these "tales of *tikkun*," we seek a healing at two different levels.

First of all, almost all our stories are retellings of some older Jewish story — in a new, more healing way. We have taken an older story — perhaps from the Torah, perhaps from the Talmud — that to our ears seemed both powerful and deeply flawed. We have told the tale again, in such a way as to heal the broken places in the older story. That is why these stories have now happened not just "once upon a time," but twice.

And secondly, we have done this to heal the wounds that fester in our wider world. For some of the original stories were not only broken, bleeding, in themselves, but in their broken edges had cut new bleeding wounds into the world. Ancient stories that left women out, or distorted their perspective, have continued to wound and weaken women in the world today. Ancient stories that honored one of the families of Abraham but denigrated another, taught enmity to the two families that has continued even to our own generation.

Some may worry that retelling a story for the sake of *tikkun* will damage the story, reduce its richness and complexity. We found just the opposite: as we danced with the ancient stories, they became richer, funnier, more nuanced, deeper. The original meanings did not vanish: new meanings grew in their midst.

This is, of course, what midrash has always done. As the ancient rabbis said, the Torah was written not in black ink on white parchment but in black fire on white fire — and in the white fire we can read the hidden places of each story. Reading the white fire — that was midrash.

These stories are new midrash. They read the white flames that dance and flicker between the words and verses where God created Shabbat, where Noah built the Ark, where Sarah and Hagar struggled with Abraham, where the midwives Shifra and Pu'ah disobeyed Pharaoh's murderous orders.

Weaving new midrashic tales within the tales of Torah is an ancient Jewish habit. We also found ourselves doing something less habitual — using the same methods to weave new tales of *tikkun* within some stories of the Talmud. The tale of that snaky "oven of Akhnai" which led to a confrontation between the majority of the rabbis and God's Own Voice in Heaven; the tale of the four rabbis who entered Paradise; the tale of Messiah's birthing on the very day the Holy Temple was destroyed — these and others we have heard speaking to us in new tongues of fire. We encourage others as well to begin doing midrash on the tales told by the rabbis.

Do these twice-told stories violate what is already in the black fire — the written text? No. The white fire enriches the original story, may even turn it topsy-turvy in a somersault — but the black fire cannot disappear, or the white fire would lose its shape. Our stories do not contradict the original text even if they are enormously expanding its horizons.

As we kept telling these stories, we realized that many of them have the form of a story within a story. We have begun to realize that the story-in-a-story is itself a sign, a symbol, an element, of *tikkun*. For sometimes it is the telling of a story that itself begins the healing of the wounded world. The Torah itself is such a story — a great long tale of healing that has moved many human beings to work toward the mending of the torn and broken world. So one way a story heals is by telling the tale of how telling a story helped to heal. Perhaps that is why the fifth book of the great tale of Torah is itself the story of how Moses told the story to the people.

Why should telling stories be so crucial to a healing? Because where there is pain and conflict, one hopeful way of getting past it at a deeper level than mere compromise is for antagonists to tell their own stories, and hear the story of the other. Simply to speak and to listen and to make clear their understanding of the other story — not to convince the other, and not to be convinced by the other. They do not have to agree; they only have to accept the honesty of each other's journeys.

And it is not just the listening that heals, but the telling itself. Each new act of imagination creates new life within the teller. Listening passively to old stories, or even to new ones, is not the point: the point is to awaken new telling in the listener, new tales of Torah from all who are walking in the path of life.

- What heals is listening to the stories that have gone before, partly for whatever truths that they contain, and partly for the seeking of the truth that they embody — and then to tell your own tales of *tikkun*. And then to listen to each other, once again.

To tell, and to listen.

To tell: "Tell it to your children on that day, saying, 'This what God — the very Breath of Life — did for me on the day when I went forth from the Narrow Place.'"

And to listen: Sh'ma! — Listen to the different voices of the One Whose tales are Infinite.

— Phyllis Ocean Berman
— Arthur Ocean Waskow
— 3d night of Hanukkah, 1995/ 5756.

# Part One
# Tales of Creation

# The Rest of Creation

ime for a rest," declared God, as the sun sank low to end day six. And as the sunset purples turned to browns and oranges, God watched the quiet and began to hum a gentle song. First the World joined in, and then all the other newly created beings: woman and man, cherry trees and turtles, ocean and night.

"What's next?" asked God. "All these six days, I have felt I was creating. Such joy! I want to do some more.

"Come," God invited the creatures. "Let's sit in a circle and help me work out the next things to create. What shall I make for day seven? And eight? And nine?"

The hippopotamus grunted, "Uh. Huh. Uh. Streams. Of water. For me. To soak in."

The bluebird gurgled, "A ribbon of blue in the sky, to match me."

The robin redbreast glared at her. "No, a ribbon of red in the sky, to match me!"

The Baltimore oriole sighed, "How about a ribbon of orange in the sky, for me-or yellow, for the canary? Or-here's the best idea-how about a ribbon in the sky of red and orange and yellow and green and blue: all the colors!"

The woman interrupted. "Wait," she said. "These all sound like nice ideas. The colors would be wonderful. But I want to tell you a story. It's about the colors, too. This afternoon in the Garden, I found some purple grapes and some red strawberries and some thick green leaves. When I squeezed them, juice came out with all the different colors. So I started to make a ... a .... " And she stopped.

"A picture," God said.

"Good word," she said, "a picture. It was beautiful. I put the juices on a flat gray rock I found in the Garden, and I began to make a picture of the Garden. With the strawberry juice, I painted a red sun, and I mixed the green and the red together to make a brown tree trunk. It felt almost like making the Garden myself." And she smiled at God.

"So I put on more and more colors," she continued. "The picture got prettier and prettier. I got really excited, and I put on one more color-and pooh! — it wasn't pretty any more! It was ruined.

"I sat and cried. I said to the picture, 'Be finished.' But the picture cried, too, and said, 'I'm just finished off.' I said to the picture, 'I'm done,' but the picture said 'I'm done in.'

"So I learned something: Before you do something more, ask yourself, is it already done? If it is, just stop. Right away. Catch your breath. Because if you don't stop when the picture is finished, you'll finish it off. If you stop when it's time to stop, you can start again when it's time — to make something new.

"So now, God, I wonder: Maybe Your world is all finished up, for now. Maybe it's time to catch Your breath. Maybe You shouldn't do any more doing."

God looked all around the circle. "Then what will I make for the seventh day?" God asked.

"You could make not making," said the man.

"That's wonderful, " said God and looked around the circle again. Then God's face began to look strange — the top like a frown, the bottom like a smile. "I see something new. You painted a picture. You told a story. You taught Me new wisdom. It really is time to rest."

"This day," God said, "will be called, 'Rest and catch your breath.' And what we'll do instead of working is — we'll sit in a circle, just as we are doing now. We'll talk, just talk, about what is work and what is rest."

"We'll sing to each other, " said the World.

"We'll breathe with each other, " said the oak tree.

"We'll dance with each other, " said the walrus.

And the bat and the bumblebee began to fly in a circle dance around each other. They went up, up, up, in a spiral of delight, while God and the oak tree breathed in and out and in and out.

"Ahhh!" said the oak tree.
''Yyyyhhhhwwwwhhhh," said God.

# The Return of Captain Noah

corching heat poured down outside the cave. The air wavered as it rose from baking rock. Within the cave, carved deep into the Ararat mountainside, all was as cool as it had been when Noah and Na'amah took apart the great Ark and packed it away, spar by spar and plank by plank.

The Voice filled the cave. "Sleepers, awake! Noah, Na'amah — I need you once again!"

From within the cave came groans and yawns and wails. What looked like blankets tossed into a heap began to stir. "Be quiet," a voice muttered; "You promised us five thousand years of sleep."

"You've already had that time, and many years

beside. I need you. The earth is threatened with a Flood once more."

"What! How can You? You promised You would never . . ."

"First of all, it isn't Me apart from you, or Me apart from all your human children. The children of the children of your children

. . . are bringing this upon themselves.

"And secondly, it's not a Flood of water this time."

"What a quibbler!. — always taking each word and letter with such care, as if you could hang an entire holocaust upon a hair of meaning! So what exactly is the danger this time?"

"See, you know it already, even when you do not know you know it! The danger is a holocaust, the burning of all things, a Flood of Fire. You say the very word even when you do not know what you are saying! You say "holocaust" ? — Even in your dreams you must have felt the flames.

"The children of the children of your children — they are obsessed with fire! Within them are burning great fires of ambition, and fire has become their symbol not of Spirit but of Action. Not of Being but of Doing. Making. The forge. The steam engine. Internal combustion — it is their own innards they are burning.

"And My innards too: My great forests they are burning. — They are making engines that burn up the coal and gasoline that long ago I wove into the earth — burn it and burn it until it chokes My air, My very Breath, with smoke and gases. — When the cities turn so hot they cannot bear it, they cool the air by using chemicals that burn great holes into My sphere of ozone. — And in their fury, they have turned whole cities into storms of fire.

"The flames they light will consume them. They have already created the first tidal waves of Smoke and Fire; soon these waves will overcome them. Yet they show no sign of stopping. Their own actions are bringing on themselves and on all living beings the Flood of Smoke and Fire.

"Awake! For you must build a safe and holy place beyond this Fire. For you, and of course for all the other life-forms.

"When the Flood of Water came, I gave you detailed instructions of how to build and enter a floating wooden Teva, the Ark of refuge. This time I call you to another sort of Teva: the Word. I bid you enter all the knowledge of the world, and I bid all that knowledge to enter within you. Take to heart all the truths that your children have discovered during your long restfulness: truths of power, energy, and science. Those truths have given so much power to your children that they can bring disaster on the earth; yet in those truths may also be the tools for you to save the bearers of all life.

"Be quiet now, and I will give you all the knowledge that has grown while you were resting."

The Voice halted, as suddenly as it had begun. Na'amah gasped:

"Wait! Wait! Hear us out before You ..."

But the Voice was not just silent. Stillness echoed through the cave, a quiet so deep that both Noah and Na'amah knew: They were on their own. And in that silence their minds were flooded with all the history and science of the last five thousand years. Behind their shut eyelids, the whole procession of human knowledge unfolded.

At last, gasping, groaning, they opened their eyes and looked at each other face to face. Na'amah shook Noah's shoulder: "Come on," she said, "I know your name means 'Restful One' but there's a limit to your resting this time! I'm not just talking sleeptime here; I am not willing to sit passively, at rest, while this Flood of Fire burns the earth and billions of the living die. It is not enough to save just a few, as we did last time. *Wake up — all the way up! We need to plan!"*

"All right," said Noah, finally. "But we can't plan alone. Too much has changed. It's far more complicated now. Even last time, do you remember how hard it was to care for the animals? Like the time the elephant tried to stamp out those red ants and stamped a hole in the Ark? How we had to beg the spiders to spin web upon crossweb to seal the hole? And nowadays — are the computers alive? Do we have to save them too? And what about the ozone layer? We need advice."

"Good thinking, Noah. Let's see . . . Last time, God gave us seven days after we had entered the Ark before the rain began to fall. I remember how frightening those seven days were, because the sun rose in the west and set in the east. Lamekh next door wept that the whole order of creation had gone into reverse — and indeed, it seemed to me a warning that God was about to "decreate" the universe, unwind the spiral of Creation. But the neighbors just wailed; they didn't use the seven days to change their ways.

"As for us, we spent the time setting the Ark to rights and finding homes aboard for all the animals. We didn't try to change our neighbors or to heal the world before disaster. This time, let us take the next seven days to seek a healing — by heeding the wisdom of seven different forms of life."

"Good thinking, Na'amah. Where shall we begin? Last time, the sea creatures were safe; the ruination that humans had brought upon the earth escaped them, and God spared them: they just lived on in the waters deep beneath the Flood. Perhaps today as well, since they are hidden in the deepest reaches of Deep Ocean, they are still of all earth's creatures the least scarred by what the humans now are doing. Safe from fire. So perhaps they have one kind of wisdom — the wisdom of those who are least frightened, least wounded.

"Let's build a canoe from these remnants of the Ark, and make our way to the Ocean Deeps to ask them."

And so Noah and Na'amah trudged down the mountainside to the nearest river, carrying planks and spars from the Ark. They canoed through whitewater rapids and floated to the sea, and then to the shores of the nearest ocean.

There Noah raised a sail, and Na'amah navigated toward the deepest deep. "You Who are the Breath of Life," they chanted, "This is Day One, and You have told us that the time is short. If You wish to save the earth then speed us onward."

And all the winds of the world, it seemed, propelled them skimming just above the waves. They quickly reached the Marianas Trench. And there they raised two conch shells, relics of the Ark, and blew ten notes of danger: three notes of alarm, long calls to rouse all beings from their torpor; three notes of wailing outcry from their memories of the Flood of Water; and three notes of broken sobbing. Then Na'amah's breath ran out, but Noah blew one long last note: "Awaaaakening!" They settled down to wait.

Three hours later, a dolphin surfaced near their boat. "I have a message from the deeps below us," she whistled and gurgled. "They say to tell you they heard your cry for help, and they ask me to carry them your message."

Said Na'amah,
"The Earth is threatened with a Flood of Smoke and Fire.
"The air is thickening, the ice is melting, the seas are rising.
"Bless us with life;
"Teach us toward a healing!"

The dolphin pirouetted, and vanished into the waves.

Three hours later, the dolphin broke from the water, rising high in a great dancing leap into the misty air. "It was hard to dive so deep," she whistled, "but when I got there I saw that everyone was dancing. The seabed is full of fantasies of life. Many of them tiny, but so different from each other! This is what they taught me —

"Dark beneath the water's shadow,
Flashing colors no one eyes.
Sheer love, overflowing joy
Dance us into many life-forms
Floating."

This is our teaching: "No barriers define us or keep us from each other, yet we multiply in our distinctiveness. If you wish to heal the earth, let love pour forth like the many flows and currents of the waters beneath waters."

Hearing this message from beneath the waves, Noah felt giddy. "Love," he laughed. "Abundance. Overflow. I see how that could save us . . . " Smiling, he stood to turn the canoe back toward shore. Smiling, he walked straight off the side of the boat, falling headfirst into the ocean.

The dolphin swam to look Noah in the face, and gurgling began to swim in circles 'round him. Every third circle, she touched her bottle nose to Noah's bald spot. He laughed and sputtered, sputtered and laughed as she hummed and strummed, splashed and leaped. Still laughing, Noah dipped beneath the waves; arose for a moment, gasping yet giggling; went under . . .

Na'amah had been smiling. But as she watched she blinked, crouched, reached carefully out with a pole of acacia wood. As Noah bobbed above the waves, he caught hold of the pole as if it were a game. He yanked. His first tug almost upended Na'amah; but she braced herself and hauled him in, arm over arm, as if she had caught some unusually smart and funny beardfish.

She eased him over the edge and he lay, gasping and guffawing, on the bottom. Na'amah turned to look at the dolphin. She was dancing in the water. Na'amah watched, delighted, and then knelt to slap a farewell into the water. "Love, abundance, overflow, and laughter," she chanted: "Fare you well." The dolphin slapped her tail and vanished.

Noah was still giggling in the bottom of the boat. "Unhinged!" Na'amah murmured. "The doors of his soul have been lifted off their hinges, and all the passageways are left wide open. Rapture of the deep."

She knelt to hold his head, kissed his eyes and ears and then his lips. "Eyes!—" she whispered: "Be screens as well as openings, choose what may enter. Ears! — Be screens as well as openings, choose what may enter. Lips! — Be screens as well as openings, choose what may enter." Noah wakened, shook his head clear, blinked and breathed and listened. He smiled at her.

Noah said, "I learned that we should treasure the overflowing energy of many forms of life. All those beings at the bottom of the sea! They are not tools for us; we did not even know that they were there. Just how many and how rich they were, that was the lesson."

Na'amah chuckled. "And how joyful. Something about the sheer liveliness made you laugh and laugh, even when you lost all boundaries and fell out of the boat. You would have fallen all the way to the bottom if I hadn't saved you!"

"I felt playful," Noah said. "Playing in the water was so much fun, I couldn't pay attention to where the water stopped or started. We humans have forgotten to be play-ful, to laugh along with life just for the pleasure of its being."

"We learned the lesson of Overflowing Love," Na'amah said. "Overflowing Love can give us overflowing life, and save the earth if we open our arms to its abun-dance; and Overflowing Love can drown our selves.

"So this is the teaching of Day One. Where shall we go to learn our second lesson?"

Na'amah spun in a slow circle to gaze upon the cir-cling world. The entire circle of the Pacific Rim came clear before her eyes. "I love it all, but love is not enough," she muttered. "Choose!" She turned the bowsprit toward the Andes Mountains.

Noah and Na'amah held hands, and once again they chanted:

"You Who are the Breath of Life: This is the Second Day, and You have told us that the time is short. If You wish to save the earth, then speed us onward."

And again the winds gathered and sped them, skimming above the waves. Swiftly there rose before them an awesome chain of snowcapped mountains, rising it seemed almost directly from the ocean.

Once again, Noah and Na'amah raised the conch shells to their lips and blew ten notes of warning. "Mountains," they called out,
"The Earth is threatened with a Flood of Smoke and Fire.
"The air is thickening, the ice is melting, the seas are rising.
"Bless us with life;
"Teach us toward a healing!
"Teach us!"

Suddenly the sea around them began to swell, and wave after wave pushed them toward the shore. The canoe touched bottom, and they walked up the sand until they stood on solid rock. The mountains towered like a great wall above them. They turned around to look back at the ocean, but suddenly the mountains seemed to close around them in an enormous stony circle.

The earth beneath them began to vibrate, and their legs began to shake. To keep themselves from falling, they sat down. Deep in their chests they began to feel words forming, slowly, one by one:
"From
us
comes
teaching

that
is
solid.

    Structure.

    Boundary.

Limit
Your
Power."

    Na'amah sat. She turned herself to look down toward the earth, her face just a few inches from the rock, staring intently . Noah watched her with a puzzled frown, and he reached a hand to touch her. She shook her shoulder impatiently, said "You stay *there*." Minute after minute passed, and Noah saw a shimmering band of light surround her. Still more silence, and then Noah heard her murmur: "We do too much.
We say too much.
We make too much,
we break too much,
we take too much."

    Her body curled into a ball. Noah waited for hours, but she seemed locked inside herself. He touched her face; it was cold and stiff. Finally he picked her up and carried her back to the boat. He set sail westward. When they passed the Isles of Spice, Na'amah breathed deeper, sneezed and sneezed again, stirred and awoke. "I need to rest here for a moment and think about what I have just been learning," she said.

"The mountains taught me about boundaries. Nowadays the human race is always slopping over, poking into everyplace. Poking holes in the ozone layer, burning up the forests. We never stop, we never rest, we never look ourselves in the face. We are always running off to somewhere else, fleeing our families and our neighborhoods. And our selves.

"What I got from those enormous mountains was amazing. They were so strong, and they weren't going anywhere. They spend thousands of years learning who they are. Suddenly I felt how strong it was to say — No further! To put a shield around myself. It gave me a stronger sense of my own depth, of what is possible inside me."

"But you went rigid, silent, icy cold. That really scared me," said Noah.

"I'm beginning to realize — our two lessons so far, each one was powerful but also carried a danger. From the ocean of Overflowing Love you almost drowned. From the mountains of Strong Boundaries I almost froze, I almost turned to stone myself.

"I'm glad you woke me," said Na'amah, putting a hand on Noah's arm. "Now where shall we go for our next lesson?"

They turned and held each other, warmed by the sun, stirred by the perfume of the Spicy Islands, quietly listening to the beating of their hearts. From deep in Noah's chest came a tickling, a hum, a purr, a gentle growling.

"Yes," said Na'amah, "I hear them too: the great black bears of Wyoming."

Noah and Na'amah held hands, and once again they chanted:

"You Who are the Breath of Life: This is the Third Day, and You have told us that the time is short. If You wish to save the earth, then speed us onward."

So their sail filled with strong new-risen winds, and swiftly they moved toward the coast of North America. When they arrived, Noah whistled and warbled in the Eagle tongue until six great bald eagles plummeted to earth. A few conversations later, Na'amah and Noah stripped down their boat, wove some grasses of the California coast into a basket large enough to hold them both, and were off into the sky — carried by the eagles over woods and deserts, lakes and mountains, until they landed in the wild Wyoming.

The eagles flew in a great circle of salute above them and thundered off.

Na'amah and Noah walked into the forest till they found a prickly patch of blackberry bushes. They gathered berries, piled them high in the woven basket of their journey, and searched the forest for the trail of bears. Then they found a clearing, placed the berries in an eight-point circle, stood in the center, and called out together in a chorus:

"Bears!

"The Earth is threatened with a Flood of Smoke and Fire.

"The air is thickening, the ice is melting, the seas are rising.

"Bless us with life;

"Teach us toward a healing!"

And they sat, cross-legged on the ground, to wait. One hour later, a bear ambled from the forest, munched some berries, and came to sit a proper distance from the couple, in the center of the circle.

"Rest," he said. And thoughtfully chewed some more.

Noah blinked. "Rest of what?"

"Not 'rest of' anything," grunted the bear. "Just 'Rest,' like 'resting.' I thought you'd understand because you were the restful one. In my tribe there are stories handed down two hundred generations of how you were always napping aboard the Ark."

Noah blushed. "I . . . I . . . " he stuttered.

"'Aye aye?' That's sailor's language, right? I wouldn't know myself, I've never sailed a ship, but the stories of the Ark — they have those salty words. 'Aye aye.'" He licked his lips. "I love something salty with these berries.

"Just rest. You people need a restful rhythm. Like me. I rest all winter. You need to set aside some time for resting. Not doing. Not making. Not using. Not breaking. Resting. Dreaming. Remembering. Reflecting.

"That's what I do all winter. I go into a cave — that part's important, it feels warm and loving. Open to thought, open to feeling, closed to enemies and frenzy. In the cave I know I can't do everything. Or anything. I don't even grow. In fact, I get thinner. But my heart-mind grows from dreaming. And when I wake up in the spring — my legs are full of new paths, my eyes are full of new visions, my guts are ready to sow new seed, even my grrrowlll has new timbre. Or is it 'timber'?" And he rose on his hind legs, grasped a slim birch tree, grrrowllled 'Timber!' and shook the whole tree, laughing as he danced.

"Your people used to rest. But now they run berserk. They never stop. They're using up these forests because they never rest.

"This Flood of Fire that you're fearful of — it's from not resting.

"Tell them to rest. Set aside some time. If they won't take off all winter, maybe a day each week, a week each month, a month each year. And make a cave. Don't run, or fly, or zip away in those smelly wheely things. They'd make nice caves if you took the wheels off. Warm, soft for making love, a place to hide some berries and some chocolate.

"My cave — it's like my heart. Each winter I go into my cave for peace and quiet, love and tenderness. Between winters I go into my heart that way: it feels like a small-sized cave, four chambers, little caverns. Quiet, calm, full of tender love."

Na'amah yawned and stretched. "You're right. I'm sleepy. Caves we know about; we've been asleep for ages in a cave. Never occurred to me that everyone could use one. Never occurred to me they could prevent the Flood of Fire. Is there a quiet cave near here?"

The bear laughed, his tongue falling all over his chin. "Of course. I'll show you. Follow me . . . Got any chocolates?" And they followed him for a nap.

The whispers of the wind lulled Noah and Na'amah into a longer sleep. They woke next afternoon. The bear was gone; out foraging for chocolates or boysenberries, maybe. Said Noah, "I've never thought of the heart, the cave, and restfulness as all the same; but I see what he means. When I dream, it does feel as if my heart is thinking — rather than my brain. We slept so long I'd almost forgotten what it was like to take a nap: It's gorgeous! So wonderful to wake up gently, nowhere to go, wriggling my toes in the luxury that there's nothing that has to be done — my heart feels open, warm, young."

"And for the world — " said Na'amah; "For the world, it is such a delicious teaching: Just pause a minute! No wonder we're in danger of a Flood of Fire! — we haven't rested for so long a time. The children of our children got so good at *making*, *doing*, that they decided resting was a waste of time. They kept running straight ahead; so of course they're on the verge of going off the cliff. We need to get them to . . . find a quiet cave, just take a nap!"

"There is one problem that I felt when I woke up," said Noah. "I really badly wanted to just keep on sleeping. Why must I worry about the Flood, and ozone, and the arsenals of fire? I could just sleep."

"I know," said Na'amah. "Remember the tale of Jonah that our Assyrian daughter-in-law, our Yaphet's wife, enjoyed to tell so often? He was a sailorman like us — that is, he learned it 'cause he had to; and the first thing he did at signs of trouble was go down into the belly of his boat to get a nap."

"I notice Black Bear does his sleeping in a rhythm," Noah said. "He sleeps the winter, but I never heard of a bear that slept through spring. I guess the point is not to overdo it. Or . . ." — he chuckled — "In this case, not to underdo it."

Na'amah stretched. "Okay, I won't. I guess I'm ready to get back to work. So where's our next learning?"

"I don't know. When you've really rested, it all looks different when you waken. New possibilities . . ."

They smiled at each other, joined hands, and once more chanted: "You Who are the Breath of Life: This is the Fourth Day, and You have told us that the time is short. If You wish to save the earth, then speed us onward."

As they walked toward the mouth of the cave, they heard a humming, thrumming. At the opening of the cave, they saw hundreds of bees. When they listened closely, they heard "Nnnnnnnnnnnoah, Nnnnna'ammmmah; Nnnnnnnnnnoah, Nnnnna'ammmmah." They looked at each other and shrugged. "Brother Bear must have told them who we are, in barter for some honey," said Na'amah. "Maybe they're our teachers for the Fourth Day. Shall we tell them why we're here?"

So together they stood just inside the cave. They chanted:
"The Earth is threatened with a Flood of Smoke and Fire.
"The air is thickening, the ice is melting, the seas are rising.
"Bless us with life;
"Teach us toward a healing!
   "Bee-swarm, teach us!"
The bees began to dance into a spiral. Listening carefully, Noah and Na'amah could hear the pattern in their buzzing. "We always have a vision of the future. When one of us finds new flowers with new nectar, we dance a spiral dance to tell the others. We spiral to make a picture of the future, when others will follow the path we have just followed. But they will enrich it: more bees, more purpose, more aiming. The spiral will rise, though its pattern will repeat us.

"And this is what the whole swarm does, across the generations. Each of us curves where the spiral requires. That is why we make a spiral dance to open our new community. We plan ahead for seven generations. Where are the flowers likely to be growing, who will nurture the Queen, shall our hive community branch in two or is there sustenance for only one?

"Your people do not look ahead. They are so starved for some honey in their lives that they drink up all the nectar, all at once. They do not brush the pollen for new flowers. And they do not ask where they might be best fitted toward the future.

"Learn to hummmm. Talk hhhummmmingly, not humanly! Humming teaches us the meaning of eternity."

Noah and Na'amah nodded. But the bee-swarm was not finished.

"You must ask your Queen to tell each worker where to work."

Noah looked up. "We have no Queen," he said.

"Yes," said the bee-swarm. "We know. That's why you're not eternal, like us. You will need to have a Queen. Perhaps we should choose a Queen for you."

"No," said Noah. Before he could explain why he was saying No, the bee-swarm was spiraling around his head. "So human!" said the swarm. "You need a Queen, but you refuse to choose one. You told us that a Flood of Fire will descend on all of earth, and yet you refuse to do what will prevent it! You refuse to do your work in the Great Swarm, and your refusal is bringing death on all of us.

"If any one of us behaved this way, the rest would sting him to death." And the swarm buzzed closer to Noah's lips and throat. Its hummm grew sharper, higher, like a snarl.

"Wait!" said Na'amah. "The Holy Breath of Life Itself has told us what our task is in the Breathing of this moment. We have learned your teaching of Eternity and Unity, and we must seek the other wisdoms that your teaching leads to. You have talked about the flowers, the source of all your nectar. Which blossoms should we learn from?"

The buzz grew calmer. "The cherry blossoms give our sweetest nectar, and their humans have the longest vision of the past and future."

"Good," said Noah and Na'amah. "We will go to study from their petals." And they hastened away from the lip of the cave, back to the woven basket of their journey. The swarm went back to building the hive.

Standing beside the woven basket, Na'amah threw back her head and shrieked. Noah jumped: "What's wrong?!" "Just letting off steam," Na'amah said. "That was a close one! Their lesson of Eternity and Unity — the lesson of planning so that we can work toward a decent future — that seems right to me. But then they turned it into Total Conformity. Not only did they want to impose a Queen on all humanity, they were ready to kill you for even questioning their edict. They are right about planning; but the place human beings have in the Great Web, the Great Swarm, is different from the place of bees. We need to bring a different kind of planning.

"I figured they wouldn't listen to anything except an appeal to their own teachers. That's why I asked for the blossoms of their honey-harvesting. I figured if I tried to argue with them, they'd sting you to death before I finished talking."

"Very smart," said Noah. "And — thank you! So now, what is the next lesson?"

"I think we should go ahead with the cherry blossoms," Na'amah said.

Na'amah threw back her head again, and this time shrieked a rhythmic series of calls into the world. Through the forest Noah heard the call repeated, echoed, and reechoed, fainter and fainter as it traveled further. Three hours later, the great bald eagles dove from the sky. They waited while Noah and Na'amah once more chanted: "You Who are the Breath of Life: This is the Fifth Day, and You have told us that the time is short. If You wish to save the earth, then speed us onward." Then they climbed into the basket, and the eagles carried it off to the slopes of Mount Fujiyama.

Noah and Na'amah found the mountain covered with cherry trees, austerely white with the palest blush of pink. They sat together at the mountain's foot, and chanted:
"The Earth is threatened with a Flood of Smoke and Fire.
"The air is thickening, the ice is melting, the seas are rising.
"Bless us with life;
"Teach us toward a healing!"
The trees whispered, hardly breathing: "Beauty!"

"What?" said Noah. — And the cherry blossoms fluttered in the wind. Noah looked deeply into them, admiring the way the barest touch of pink gently deepened into the heart of the flower until it became a spark of burgundy.

"Fearing disaster — that is not enough," whispered the blossoms. "You will never heal the earth if all you feel is fear of its destruction.

"Pursuing justice — even that is not enough," whispered the blossoms. "You will never heal the earth if all you seek is justice for its weakest species."

"Delighting in beauty — that you also need," whispered the blossoms. "You need to wander in the forests and the deserts, the tundra and the thunder. You need to see and hear how delicate we are and how profoundly piercing; you need to sniff our spice and salt and taste our fiery peppers.

"Then! — To the bees' rhythmic march of earnest planning toward eternal fruitfulness, you will add our flowering melodies of joy, delight."

Noah looked deeper into the cherry blossom in his hand. Deeper into a single petal. Its shadings drew him even deeper: palest pink and richest red and warmest white. One raindrop shimmered on the petal's surface, and in that raindrop quivered all the universe. In that raindrop shimmered all the rich reds, pale pinks, warm whites of Na'amah's loving, curving breast; all curving, flowing earth, and every whirling galaxy; each crawling beetle as it curved its path beneath the tree trunk, and each soaring eagle as it carved its curving flight across the heavens; all the spiral of birthing, dying life. The colors moved and stirred within him as the raindrop trembled on the petal's edge and then slid gently toward the blossom's heart.

Dimly he felt a warmness on his arm. It spread: the slant and slide of warmth growing as gently on his skin as the slant and slide of color had moved into his eyes. As his forearm felt a faint caress grow stronger, his hand, his shoulder, his chest, felt the blood stir warmer. Slowly his eyes and heart released the cherry blossom, slowly he turned to see what warmth was moving from his arm into his body. Slowly his eyes adjusted to a different scale of vision, and he saw a hand just touching him. His whole body shook, his breathing quickened, and he saw Na'amah's hand upon his upper arm.

His lips shook, his tongue rustled before he could shape his mouth into a question. "What?" he said, and turned to see Na'amah's face crinkle into a smile. "Thank God, and welcome!" she murmured. He blinked — the raindrop on the cherry blossom reappeared for an instant in his eyes — and said, "Where have I been?"

"*When* have you been is nearer to the question," Na'amah said. "You've been right here, and for two hours you've been inside that flower. I thought perhaps I'd lost you to the melodies of color."

"Almost," he said. "I thought you were in there with me. Your hand, your breast . . ." She smiled, and her lips curled into the blossom of the cherry. For a moment he floated away again, felt her hand tighten again, shook himself into her hand again.

"So even beauty has its cost," he said. "I could have fallen deeper and deeper, never have come back to heal the world because one flower was touching me so deeply."

Na'amah nodded. Noah sighed. "So our journey isn't over," he muttered. " Where do we go from here?"

"Each day, our lesson for that day has moved us into the next one," said Na'amah. "What saved you when you fell into the flower — what saved us all — was my hand, reaching out to touch you and awaken you. We connected."

They smiled at each other, joined hands, and once more chanted: "You Who are the Breath of Life: This is the Sixth Day, and You have told us that the time is short. If You wish to save the earth, then speed us onward."

"But where do we go from here?" said Noah. "Where are we speeding?"

"We aren't," said Na'amah. "I think the lesson is connecting. And who connects better than human beings? We are the creatures of reaching-out. Our young stay helpless for years, so that they need a community of people who reach out to care for them. And we talk and talk and talk, reaching out to others with our lips and tongues."

Noah laughed, and kissed her: "Well, that's for sure!"

"So we are the people that we seek," Na'amah laughed behind his kisses. "If the Breath of Life needs to speed us toward each other, it's only in our understanding — not our bodies."

"In our bodies, too!" said Noah, kissing her again.

"That's true. This is a better way to say it: we need to touch with our minds and our feelings the way we do with our bodies. When we talk, we need to use the words as if we were making love. And when we learn from the world around us, just as we've been doing, it has to be a kind of learning that is also like making love."

"It used to be that way," said Noah. "When we got off the Ark, I remember that I didn't just plant a grapevine — I invited the grapevine to its own harvest party. Such a time we had that night!"

Na'amah made a face. "Yes, I remember — and I remember how drunk you got, you and your grapes!"

"True, I overdid it. Still, I didn't bring a Flood of Fire on us. One of the reasons we're in danger now is that too many of the humans have been acting as if the world were dead already. If they want to understand a grapevine, do they invite it to the party? No! They poke coldly at it, pick it apart, dissect it without ever connecting to it. They treat it like a cold dead corpse. If we treat the world as if it's dead, it dies — and we die with it!"

"I understand!" said Na'amah. "Truly, I understand what you are saying. What I don't understand is why you keep saying it. I feel as if you're lecturing me, when I already know what's wrong. Next thing you know, you'll be calling out our mission, our outcry, to me — as if I didn't know it."

"You're right, you're right!" said Noah. "Let's hear each other say it!

"The Earth is threatened with a Flood of Smoke and Fire.
"The air is thickening, the ice is melting, the seas are rising.
"Bless us with life;
"Teach us toward a healing!"

"I get it — really, I get it!" said Na'amah. "I got it long ago. You're making reaching-out barely bearable. Here we are, just two of us, and yet it feels to me as if you're standing on a skyscraper and shouting out your lecture. Maybe there are moments for the skyscraper, but the whole idea of asking for advice is more like gathering around a tiny table. If people are going to receive your out-reaching, they need to have some space to breathe, to think their own thoughts and speak their own amendments to your manifesto. Maybe something new will come of how they react to what you say!"

Noah looked dazed, his face red, his body arched into space, every limb pointing outward. "Reach out, reach out!" he muttered.

Na'amah gathered his body in her arms. "Receive, receive," she murmured. He began to tremble, to quiver, and gradually his muscles softened. Na'amah helped him to sit down.

"Whoosh!" said Noah. "Almost lost it there. From a good thing, too — from reaching out. It's so easy to get drunk on a good thing, the way I got drunk on those grapes last time we sailed the Ocean."

"Well of course," said Na'amah. "Who would get drunk on something that felt bad?"

Noah laughed. "It's been that way with every lesson, no? First we get to like it, then it slops over. I guess there's such a thing as too much out-reaching, or a too tense way of reaching out. It's the nature of out-reaching to be a lit-

tle tense — just feel your body when it's reaching out."
And he stretched his whole body, arched up and out and
over. He shuddered.

"And not just out-reaching. Funny how each lesson
has a dark side too. How do we guard against getting
drunk on the dark side, whatever it is? Each lesson acts
as a corrective to the others — but not just a corrective,
not just saying 'No.' Each one says 'Yes' to the best part
of the others.

"I think . . . I think . . . we need to gather all our
teachers, so that each one works to strengthen the best of
the others. Connect, then collect!"

·   "Time for the Seventh Day?" said Na'amah. "Are we
agreeing — this time we're meeting with all the other
teachers?"

They smiled at each other, joined hands, and once
more chanted: "You Who are the Breath of Life: This is the
Seventh Day, and You have told us that the time is short. If
You wish to save the earth, then speed us onward."

"Whoops," said Noah. "Onward *whither*? Where are
we gathering?"

"It will take a special place, a unique time, to make
this possible," said Na'amah. "We are so different from
each other — the Bear and the Mountain, the Ocean's
Deep-Life and the Cherry Blossoms, the Bee-swarm and
the two of us — there is no ordinary place and time where
we can meet. The Holy Breath of Life left us on our own;
but now we need to go beyond our ordinary lives."

Around them the wind gathered strength, and hints of words began to stir in the breezes. Suddenly above them there glowed in the sky the great Arc of the Rainbow. The whispering wind became a clearer Voice: "My Bow of seven colors I grant you for this Seventh Day. Beneath the Bow, beyond time and space, in the day that is a whisper of eternity, I affirm the gathering of all your teachers."

Suddenly the earth dropped away beneath the feet of Noah and Na'amah, and the wind bore them into somewhere deeper than a darkened violet. The Rainbow doubled and became a great and glowing circle full of color. Within the circle there appeared another circle, the teachers of the first six days: a cluster of exotic flowering plants and tiny animals awash in waves of briny water; a towering mountain topped with snow; a panting, laughing black bear; a buzzing spiral of swarming honeybees; a cherry tree bearing curves of pale blossoms dusted with a hint of pink; Noah and Na'amah. Under the great Arch swooped and danced a band of eagles; beneath them, in what might have been dark water or night air, a single dolphin played with an acacia-wood canoe and a woven basket.

"So you have gathered us," hummed the bees. "What do you want?"

"Simply to celebrate your gifts together," Na'amah said.

"The Earth is threatened with a Flood of Smoke and Fire.

"The air is thickening, the ice is melting, the seas are rising.
"Bless us with life;
"Teach us toward a healing!"
"What are our wisdoms?" hummed the bees.
Chanted Noah and Na'amah in a lilting unison:
"From the oceans, overflowing love;
"From the mountains, structured boundaries;
"From Brother Bear, a focus for compassionate restfulness;
"Planning for eternity, from the bees,
"And from the cherry blossoms, playful graceful beauty in
the moment;
 "Connecting;
"Collecting."

And all the creatures whirled as the colors of the
great Bow turned to a symphony of sound: red shrill and
piercing voices of a flute, an indigo bass viol, a trumpet's
golden shining.

"Here begins the healing of each Self and all of
Earth," they heard the Breath of Life beneath the chorus.

# Part Two
# Tales of Love and Freedom

# Why Hagar Left

ong ago and far away is where most stories start; indeed, most of the stories that we tell together in this book. But this tale begins in our own lives — in Phyllis' own life. And so she tells it —

One day when I was sixteen, I came home from school very upset. My mother asked me what was wrong. I told her that Danny, the-love-of-my-life, was spending a lot of time with my second-best-friend Tamar. And I was frightened. I could only see Danny on weekends because he went to a different high school; but Tamar got to see him all the time — at school and at their synagogue's youth group. At the moment they were only friends, but I knew that Tamar really liked Danny, and I knew that he was also interested in her.

"So you're jealous of her?" said my mother.

"Well, of course," I said. "What else can I feel? I'm worried I'll lose him; in fact, I'll lose them both."

"Where did you get the idea that two women have to compete over a man?" my mother asked with a sparkle in her eyes.

Incredulously, I blurted out, "Come on! From the time I was an infant, I've gone to shul; from the time I started Hebrew school, I've read the Chumash. We hear the story of the competition between Sarah and Hagar not just once but twice a year in the Torah reading cycle. It's all about jealousy over Abraham's affection! How can you ask me that question so innocently? I've been taught jealousy and competition from my birth."

"And from your birth, I've been waiting to have this conversation with you," my mother said, patting the chair beside her to invite me to sit down. "But I had to wait till you were ready — more than ready. So at last it's time; at last it's clear you need to hear what I'm about to say.

"What you've been learning — it's not the whole story. How do I know? My mother told me when I was about your age; she had heard it from her mother, who had heard it from her mother, all the way back through all the generations. What she told me is the *real* story of Sarah and Hagar . . ."

Sarai and her boyfriend Avram — those were their names until late in their life — grew up in the same little town. Not only were they cousins, they were friends from childhood. So it was no surprise to anyone when their friendship turned to love.

Most of the young folks they knew stayed close to home, even when the time had come to marry. But Avram and Sarai were different. Sarai heard the words over and over, as if in a dream: "L'chi lach" — "Leave where you are, to learn who you are."

So she and Avram left their families and their home town and all that was familiar to them, to make their new life together.

As they journeyed, they came to a town where a powerful Pharaoh was in charge. At first it seemed a good place to live, because land was plentiful for grazing cattle and growing crops. But Sarai and Avram quickly noticed that, while there were some men in the area, there were no other women to be seen.

Avram made some discreet inquiries and learned that all of the town's women were living under the Pharaoh's "protection" in his palace. Even worse — in the past, some men had protested when the Pharaoh's officers had come to take the women to the palace. Those men had simply disappeared. The whisper was they were most likely dead.

"We should never have left home!" Avram thought. Night after night, he woke up trembling: Pharaoh might kill him too, in order to add Sarai to his conquests.

So one morning Avram said to Sarai, "If Pharaoh asks us, we'll tell him you're my sister."

"I suppose it's almost true," said Sarai. "You are my

cousin. And I love that song you used to sing to me — "How sweet is your love, my sister, my bride!" She looked into his frightened face. "All right; I'm willing."

Sure enough, not long after that the Pharaoh asked about them. Learning they were siblings, he ordered Sarai into his harem. As you can imagine, Sarai was terrified: she was separated from her beloved Avram and didn't know what was going to happen to her. So she looked around for a friend, and quickly found another young woman, who only weeks before had herself been added to the collection of Pharaoh's women. And she was a foreigner too, from a distant city — so far away that the other women called her "Hagar" (The Stranger).

So Sarai and Hagar, both far from home, uncertain when they'd be released or what would happen until then, both new to the palace culture, became immediate and intimate friends.

Now when the Pharaoh had first approached Avram and Sarai, he had promised that she'd be free of her palace duties and able to return to Avram's home after a year. And so he said to all the women before they entered his palace. But when Sarai and Hagar looked around, they could see women of all ages. It looked to them as though women were remaining in the harem far more than the single year they had expected.

When they asked the other women how long they had lived in the palace, they heard the same story over and over again. Yes, the Pharaoh had said they might leave after a year, but, by that time, each of them had borne a child. The Pharaoh told them they could leave if they wanted to; but the child, his child, must remain in the palace. What woman, each one said in her own way, could walk away from a child still nursing at the breast? So the single year of servitude turned into many years, the child into children, and after awhile they could no longer extricate themselves from the Pharaoh's home.

The key to freedom, Sarai and Hagar said to each other, is not to become pregnant during this year. But how could they avoid it when none of the other women had been able to? They thought and thought, they talked and talked. And finally they remembered that, in their own home towns, there had been a special feast at the sighting of the new moon each month. In the women's community where Sarai came from, it was called "Rosh Chodesh." The women talked through the night, one idea melting into another until they had the perfect plan.

The next day the two women gained audience with Pharaoh, who was delighted to receive the newest additions to his harem. They told him how it was the custom in their traditions to celebrate the new moon: he should invite all the men in his retinue to a monthly feast which would be prepared, not by the royal cooks and bakers, but by all the women themselves. The Pharaoh so much liked the idea of a monthly gathering of men to eat and drink that he hardly thought twice when the women mentioned that, once the food and wine were prepared, the women

would go off into the woods by themselves for a night or
two, to celebrate the moon's fecundity.

"Ah, but that night or two was crucial!" my mother
said. "When you live with other women in a college dor-
mitory, you'll see. For when many women live together,
they often begin to menstruate on the same cycle. And in
those days when there were no electric lights, women's
cycles, like the tides, mirrored the rhythms of the moon
as it waxed and waned each month. Those days of the
New Moon — that was when the women were most fer-
tile!"

Sarai and Hagar knew that, if the women were out
of the palace and away from Pharaoh during the most fer-
tile point of their month, they would probably not get
pregnant. And for some months, the plan worked very
well indeed. None of the women got pregnant — and
Pharaoh didn't even notice. That was because there were
still women who had already become pregnant before the
New Moon celebrations started. They kept having babies.
Pharaoh and his men reveled in the feasts, eating and
drinking the finest specialties of the women's dishes.

For Sarai and Hagar, the months passed joyfully,
each new moon another step toward their day of freedom.
Each month, they felt safer from a lifetime sentence.

Four months, five months, six months — and
Pharaoh realized something strange was happening. No
morning sickness, no bellies swelling. What had happened
to halt all fertility?

And then one afternoon, when Avram made his weekly visit into the ruler's gardens where he could talk and walk with his "sister" Sarai, the Pharaoh just happened to be standing on his balcony.

Sarai and Avram were deep in conversation. Now you know how it is, when two people love each other — how they look at one another, how they touch. Even from the distance of his balcony, the Pharaoh could see in the energy field of their loving glance, that this was not the look that one would expect between a brother and a sister. He began to think about life in his palace in the recent months, and suddenly all the different pieces of information fell into place. He ordered Avram and Sarai to his presence immediately.

"You lied to me," the Pharaoh roared. "Anyone can see you are husband and wife, not brother and sister."

"In our tradition," Avram said, "it is common to refer to our brides as our sisters. This is merely a misunderstanding," he assured the Pharaoh. "Even our poetry . . ."

"Poetry, shmoetry! You have bewitched my Kingdom with your trickery! "said Pharaoh. "I have been cursed with infertility since you have come here. Get out of my palace and away from my lands this instant, and let us return to our blessed state of birthing many babies."

Avram was ready to leave immediately, but Sarai balked. "I'm not leaving here without my dear friend Hagar," she said determinedly, looking the Pharaoh in the eye.

"You are lucky to get out of here with your lives," Pharaoh fumed. "Take Hagar," he said; "just get yourselves out of here and leave us in peace."

And that is how it happened that the companions Sarai and Hagar, and the couple Sarai and Avram became a family of three. It was no surprise that just as Sarai loved both Avram and Hagar, so it was that Avram and Hagar came to love one another as well. The three settled in Hebron and peacefully went on with their lives.

Well — *mostly* peacefully, because for several years neither Sarai nor Hagar became pregnant. "Maybe our trick has brought a curse on both of us?" they worried. They prayed together: "You Who are the Source of All Life and all Liberty, You Who heard our prayers for freedom from the Pharaoh's palace, hear our prayers for new life now."

So it was an enormous relief when Hagar's belly did begin to swell. When the son of Hagar and Avram was born, the three called his name "Yishmael — God hears," for God had listened to their prayers. If you've seen how dear friends or close family members delight in the birth of one another's children, so it was with Sarai, who adored Yishmael as fully as Hagar and Avram did. There's more than enough work for two mothers when a newborn comes into a family, and Sarai was involved with Yishmael's parenting in every way but one.

The one thing that Sarai could not do was to nurse the baby, and, according to my mother, when Sarai watched Hagar soothe and satisfy the baby at her breast, it caused her some grief. She yearned for a baby born from her own body, but in all other ways she loved Yishmael as her own.

The household flourished; living together was easy; and the years passed. Sarai had almost made her peace with the fact that her body would bear no children when their household was visited by three strange-seeming guests. First the three suggested that both Sarai and Avram slow down and breathe more. They even urged them both to add a breathing sound to their names as a reminder: "Sarahhh and Avrahham." And if they were to do that, the visitors predicted, within the year Sarai herself would give birth to a son.

Sarai laughed to hear such news. "After all these years?" she said — in a mixture of joy and disbelief. Yet, filled with hope, she and Avram agreed to rename themselves as the visitors had suggested: Sarah and Avraham.

Now you may think that everything was finally perfect, but I'm sorry to say that a strange shadow fell upon the family right before the birth of Sarah's baby. Avraham awoke one morning full of dreams about a commanding transcendent lordly God. In his dreams he had heard this God demand the circumcision of all the males in the family — the adolescent Yishmael, the aging Avraham, and all future newborn boys — to hallow the male genitals to create life for ongoing generations.

Avraham told these words to Sarah and Hagar, and the women were outraged. "You mean to say that you'd take our Yishmael — a thirteen-year old just coming to terms with his body's change from boyhood to manhood — and you want to cut off the skin at the tip of his penis?" Hagar said incredulously.

"Yes," Avraham answered, "I, and all the men of our clan and our village, and all the boy children, including our Yishmael, must be circumcised.

"For God insists that on the eighth day of life we will circumcise newborns, but now we must consecrate men and boys of all ages so that our people will be as numerous as grains of sand on the seashore or stars in the sky."

The women looked at each other in disbelief. They could barely tolerate the thought of maiming their male child, let alone the men in the community. It made no sense, they thought; and yet, Avraham was so certain that it was what God wanted. Finally and reluctantly, they agreed, and the circumcisions were done.

But from that moment on, a gulf fell open between the two women and Avraham. If he could dream such weird dreams, such dangerous and outrageous dreams, who knew what might be next?

And yet all this was put aside when Sarah delivered a healthy baby boy. To this son, the three of them gave the name "*Yitzhak* — Laughing One," because the news of his coming had caused all of them to laugh with delight.

The family of five continued to grow in love and

prosperity, until one morning Sarah awoke from a terrible night's dream. She was so distressed that she told it to Hagar: In her nightmare, Avraham had had another dream. This time God had told him to take his first-born son to a nearby mountain, and, like so many of their neighbors who believed that sacrificing living beings insured continued fertility, sacrifice him. As Sarah told the dream, she began to cry. Her body shook and her voice broke.

Hagar put her arms around Sarah. "Beloved Sarah, it is just a dream," said Hagar.

"Beloved Hagar, it is just a dream," said Sarah.

"It is just a dream of a dream," said each woman to the other.

But the dream came to Sarah once again, and yet once more. "Three times!" she said to Hagar. "It will no longer leave me in the morning. Remember when Avraham dreamed that God wanted our oldest son circumcised? Is it so impossible that he might dream that God wants him to sacrifice our oldest son?"

Sarah and Hagar didn't know what to think; but, since the circumcision, they were not so confident about Avraham and the voices he chose to listen to. "What can we do if Avraham decides to take our Yishmael to sacrifice him?" they cried. And so they sat and talked and planned and plotted through the day and into the night, just as they had done so many years before, in the Pharaoh's palace.

And once again, they agreed on an idea, this time to protect Yishmael from Avraham's potential dream. The plan, my mother said, is one we know well; it's the one we read about in the Torah. If Sarah were to tell Avraham this preposterous story about Yishmael teasing Yitzhak and demand that Avraham send Yishmael and Hagar away from the household, he would have to believe her, because he knew without a doubt how bound together the women and the boys had been. So he would send Hagar and Yishmael away.

It was a terrible plan, a heartbreaking one, but one that would keep Yishmael alive and out of Avraham's reach.

We all know what happened: Sarah did tell Avraham that she and Yitzhak could no longer stand to live with Hagar and Yishmael. Avraham couldn't understand it, but Sarah was so insistent that Avraham agreed, with a heavy heart, to send them away.

The night before Hagar and Yishmael were to go, the two women sat up, alternately weeping and reminiscing, and, each in her own hand, they wrote two scrolls. In each was the real story of their love and friendship through all the years they had lived together. Hagar placed her scroll in Sarah's hands, to give to a daughter-in-law or other female relative. Sarah put her parchment in Hagar's hands for the same purpose.

So it was that Hagar and Yishmael left the household and went out into the desert. How they survived there and made a life for themselves is a story for another day. It's enough to say that they lived a good and long life. Yishmael had many children and won a great deal of respect among those with whom he settled.

Sarah was never the same after Hagar and Yishmael went their own way. She became withdrawn and lonely, barely consoling herself with mothering the growing Yitzhak. Although she believed that her deception had saved Yishmael's life, it had taken from her most of her own life energy.

You can imagine, then, how shocked, how outraged she was, many years later when Avraham, indeed, did have the dream she had seen in her own vision. For in his dream, Avraham did hear God commanding him to take his son, his only son, his beloved son Yitzhak up to Mount Moriah and to sacrifice him there. Avraham did take Yitzhak, and was ready to sacrifice him on that day. But at the last moment, God sent a ram to take Yitzhak's place on the altar.

When Avraham and Yitzhak returned home after this terrifying journey, Sarah was on her deathbed, grief-stricken once more and half-crazed that everyone she had ever loved would be lost to her. When she saw that Yitzhak had returned, miraculously alive, she blessed him and gave him the parchment that had been written by Hagar.

"This scroll," Sarah said, "is my gift to your wife if you should marry. I don't expect to live long enough to give it to her myself, but there is a story she and her off-spring must know."

So it was, my mother told me, that Yitzhak present-ed Rivkah with this mysterious gift from his mother Sarah; Rivkah eventually gave it to her daughter-in-law Leah, who gave it to her daughter Dina, and so it passed from generation to generation through the ages. When the actual scrolls disappeared, women just told the story to their daughters and granddaughters, to their nieces and their cousins.

Through this whole story, my mother and I had been sitting side by side, Her eyes were turned more inward, toward the past, than facing me. But now she took my arm and turned the two of us to face each other. And then she said, "At last this story I've so longed to tell you — at last I can put this story in your hands. Now it is your responsibility to pass on to the next generation, so people will know the truth about Sarah and Hagar.

"And more!" — she said. "Now you too can look beyond the world of jealousy and competition. You can ask yourself whether we must forever live according to the tale you learned in school — or has the time begun to come when women can shape the world together, as Hagar and Sarah tried to do."

# The Long Narrow
# Pharaoh and the
# Pass-Over People

ong long ago, there was a looong thin river. Along its banks there was a looong thin country. The country was ruled by a looong thin King.

He was so famous for being long and thin that when people spoke directly to him, they called him "Your Royal Longness."

But his name was "Pharaoh," and behind his back, they called him "Narrow Pharaoh."

Pharaoh was long and narrow because he didn't like to eat.

"Eating is fun," he said. "And kissing is fun. And laughing is fun. Being a king is serious. It is not supposed to be fun!

"Long and narrow is serious," he said. "But eating makes bulges. Bulges are not serious.

"No more bulges!" said the long narrow Pharaoh.

"I am long and narrow,

"My kingdom is long and narrow,

"And all my people shall become long and narrow!

"When I am not eating, no one shall eat.

"When I am not kissing, no one shall kiss.

"When I am not laughing, no one shall laugh."

One morning, Narrow Pharaoh looked out the window. There was a chubby little baby laughing in the grass.

The King began to frown. "Babies make bulges, too," he said.

"If you put a baby in a long thin woman, you make a bulge in her.

"If you put too many babies in a long thin country, you make a bulge in the country.

"I hate babies!" said the long thin King.

"They cry when I am not sad,

"And they smile when I am not happy.

"They eat when I am not hungry,

And they smell — all the time!"

So Narrow Pharaoh went to his high high throne.

Up the steps he walked — five steps, eleven steps, seventeen steps.

When he looked very very tall, and very very thin,
he spoke in a very narrow voice:

"Send me my Minister of Exact Justice!"

The Minister stalked in.

He was almost as thin as the King,

And his clothes were even thinner.

He was almost as tall as the King,

And his hat was even taller.

Said Narrow Pharaoh, "Tell me how to get rid of
these extra babies!"

The Minister of Exact Justice raised an exactly shaped
eyebrow. He raised it exactly three-eighths of an inch.

"Let the babies grow up to be children," the Minister
said. "Then you'll be rid of them!"

"No!" said Pharaoh. "What good will it do if they're
children? The children don't do what I say.

"They keep silent when I say 'Speak up!'

"And they whisper when I call for 'Silence!'

"They kiss when I say 'Hands off!'

"They loaf when I say 'Get your work done!'

"And — they eat when I am not hungry!"

"Let the children grow up to be grown-ups," said the
Minister.

"No!" said the King.

"What good will it do if they're grown-ups?

"The grown-ups do what I say,

"But they laugh at the strangest times.

"They work when I say 'Work harder!'

"But they laugh when I say, 'I work hardest of all!'

"They fight when I say, 'Join the army!'

"But they laugh when I say, 'Death is glory!'

"They pay taxes when I say 'Make my palace richer!'

"But they laugh when I say, 'If my own bed is soft, everyone sleeps better.'

"It's good to have a big audience when I give speeches on the balcony," he said

"But there are so many people they start talking ... with each other."

"It's good to have lots of soldiers when I need to march across the border," he said.

"But there are so many soldiers they might even join . . . with each other. And rebel against me!

"There are just too many people for my long thin Kingdom.

"Tell me, Minister — get it right!

What to do to win this fight."

And he glared hard at his Minister of Exact Justice.

The Minister's eyes turned gray, and his lips turned gray. He spoke very fast: "Get-rid-of-the-extra-people!"

"Oh," said the long thin King. "Now that would be exactly perfect! Why didn't you say so before?" And he threw a blanket over the Minister's head before he could speak any more.

\* \* \*

Then the long thin King called out in his narrow voice:

"Send my Minister of Exact Numbers!
"Tell me, Minister Thin and Tight,
"How to get these numbers right.
"How many people are extra?"

So the Minister opened his Number File. Out came tumbling lists of numbers. Numbers of soldiers, and numbers of houses. Numbers of taxes, and numbers of milk bottles. Numbers of bed sheets and numbers of numbers. Innumerable numbers!

The Minister looked at all his numbers. He added them up and divided by 12, got a square root and subtracted 4.

"Exactly six hundred thousand extra people," he finally said.

"In that case, Your Majesty," said the Minister of Exact Justice in a muffled voice from under the blanket, "I know exactly what to do. Up in the north are the Cross-Over people. "Just four hundred years ago, a small band of them crossed over the Sea of Blood and started roaming around our country. They never settle down. They keep crossing over the Great Desert — coming here, crossing back, crossing here, going back.

"When we treat them like foreigners, they get very cross. And when we treat them like home-folks, they get very cross. So that's why we call them the Cross-Overs.

"They have lots of babies." (Narrow Pharaoh turned slightly green.)

"They have lots of children." (Narrow Pharaoh turned slightly red.)

"And their grown-ups laugh a lot at the strangest times." (Narrow Pharaoh turned slightly purple.)

"So they have grown and grown and grown. Last week there were exactly twelve hundred thousand of them. You could get rid of half — and that would be exactly correct."

"If they're so cross, let's double-cross them!" said the King — and he snickered.

So Narrow Pharaoh looked down from his very high throne. "Time to act," said Pharaoh sharply. "Which half of the Cross-Overs should I get rid of?"

And he glared at the Minister of Exact Numbers, who got out a page of records and began to read very nervously: "Half of them are grown-ups, and half of them are children. Half of them are women, and half of them are men. Half of them have black hair, and half of them have red hair. Half . . ."

"STOP!" said Pharaoh. "I know! I'll get rid of the men. The men make trouble. The men are strong, And the men are always laughing. And the men ask questions when I tell them what to do.

"But the women are pretty, and they do what I say."

The Minister of Exact Justice frowned.

He opened his mouth to tell the King that the women might not just do what he said.

But the King was grinning. His grin was so wide the Minister thought the top of his head might come off.

So the Minister closed his mouth, and looked extremely worried.

"Now!" said the King. "Get me the Minister of Medicine."

"Tell me, Minister, Long and Thin,
"How to get rid of the Cross-Over men!"

"Start with the babies," the Minister said.

The King's face lit up; he felt even happier.

Said the Ministers:

"Bring in the midwives
"Who help mothers give birth
"To their babies.
"Tell them to drown
"All the boys
"As soon as they're born.
"After a while
"There won't be any men!"

So Narrow Pharaoh clapped his hands. In came two women — named Shifra and Pu'ah.

"Tell me, women long and thin . . ." the King began.

But then his voice faltered. He looked again at the women. They weren't especially long, and they weren't especially thin. Especially Shifra — who was short and schmaltzy.

Narrow Pharaoh looked itchy. Then he shrugged. "Kill all the boy-babies of the Cross-Over people as soon as they're born!" said Pharaoh. "As for the girls and the women — let them alone. They're too weak to matter."

Shifra and Pu'ah looked at each other. "Pooh!" whispered Pu'ah. "Who said we're so weak?"

"Shhh," whispered Shifra. "Are you so sure we're strong?

"This is no time for talking. If we're strong, we can show it by acting."

So they bowed to Pharaoh. Then they stepped backward and backward until they were out of the Throne Room.

* * *

Shifra and Pu'ah walked down a long thin hallway and out the palace door.

"It makes me sad," said Pu'ah. "But I suppose the King is the King. We're supposed to do what he says.

"Maybe he knows what he's doing. Maybe he has facts we don't have. There must be something bad about the Cross-Over people. Or bad about boys."

Shifra shivered, and they kept walking through a great broad meadow, scattered with trees — oranges and bananas, plums and quinces. They kept walking through the meadow till it ended at a riverbank. When they got close, Shifra looked at the river and laughed.

"I thought the river was long and thin —

"But now I see it is broad.

"It wanders and curls and bulges.

"I can hear it laughing — at Pharaoh!

"I can hear it singing —

" 'The Pharaoh is Narrow,

" 'And the river broad.'

"I think we should learn from this water."

Pu'ah reached up to a plum tree. Its leaves rustled in the wind, and she leaned very close to hear its whispering. "The tree is breathing!" said Pu'ah, and a plum fell, plop, at her feet. "I think we should learn from this breathing," said Pu'ah.

So Shifra sat quietly listening to the river, and Pu'ah sat quietly, listening to the wind. The two of them sat still for so long that a messenger ran up to say: "There's a Cross-Over woman who needs your help to give birth!"

Shifra stood up. She took Pu'ah's hand. Together they walked slowly down the riverbank till they came to the Cross-Over village.

The mother was sitting in an open hut. Its roof was made of branches, and the walls were full of flowers. The mother shook and grunted and yelled. Shifra gently rubbed her back.

Pu'ah said, "The wind will teach us. Breathe deep. Breathe deeeep. Breathe slow. Breathe sloooow. Breathe deeeep. Breathe sloooow. Breathe deeeep . . ."

Shifra said nothing, but when the birth waters broke she said, "The river will teach us," and held out her hands for the baby.

The baby was born — a boy. Tears of joy poured from

the mother's eyes, and the baby began to suck at her breasts, to drink her milk.

Shifra looked at Pu'ah. Pu'ah looked at Shifra. Together they walked a little way off. They looked at the mother and the baby.

Shifra finally spoke:

"I am trying to see the King's face, but I can only see the mother's face. I see her face every which way. Tears of joy. Tears of sadness. The flow of the river in her eyes."

Pu'ah finally spoke:

"I am trying to hear the King's voice, but I can only hear the baby's cry. I hear his voice over and over. Giggling, gurgling, the flow of the wind in his breathing."

Shifra listened to the mother suckling.

Pu'ah listened to the baby breathing.

"The King is strong," said Pu'ah, "but this breathing is still stronger."

"The King is rich," said Shifra, "but this suckling is much richer."

"May this breath of life be King forever and ever," said Pu'ah.

And suddenly around them everywhere they heard The Breath of Life. The palm trees were breathing. The crocodiles were breathing. The cat was breathing. The dandelions were breathing. The moon was breathing. Everything was breathing. The breathing sounded like this: "Yyyy-hhhh-wwww-hhhh."

"I will not stop this breath," said Pu'ah.

"I will not stop this breath," said Shifra.

And they turned and tiptoed out of the hut and out of the village.

* * *

Eight days later, Pharaoh sent for Shifra and Pu'ah. When they entered the Throne Room, his face was angry and purple.

"There are still boy babies in the Cross-Over villages!" he said.

Shifra and Pu'ah reached out to hold hands.

"I am a woman, and the mother was a woman," said Shifra "I could not kill her baby."

"I breathe, and the baby breathes," said Pu'ah. "I will not take away his breath."

"I can take away *your* breath!" said Pharaoh.

"You can take away our breath," said Pu'ah. "But the whole world breathes. The King breathes, and the kingdom breathes. In and out, up and down. Now you are up. But you will come down. If you stop our breathing, then your breathing will stop. The Kingdom will stop."

"You can kill these births," said Shifra. "But the whole world is born. The King is born, and the Kingdom is born. If you stop birthing, you will have no more births. Your aborning will die. The Kingdom will die."

"But I am the King. I can kill the whole kingdom. I can kill the Cross-Over people, and everyone else besides."

"No, you can't," said Shifra and Pu'ah. "We will not

do it. No one will do it. We will help them to breathe, we will help them to live."

"There are too many of them already!" said the King. "My Kingdom is full of them. We are tight, we are narrow, we have no space!"

"Then let them come out from your Narrow Place, and let them break through the Red Waters, and let them be born! We are midwives. We know it is time for a birth."

"I will not! I will kill all of them, and I will start out with you!" said the King. "I will throw you in the sea to drown in its waters, I will cast you into the desert to die in its wind storms!"

"We are people of birth, not people of death," said Shifra. "We will come to the sea and its waters will break, and we will pass through them aborning. Death will pass over us!"

"We are people of breath, not people of death," said Pu'ah. "We will breathe in the desert and death will pass over us all!"

Pharaoh looked hard at them. They looked hard at Pharaoh. They turned to walk out of the room.

But Pharaoh began to laugh. His laugh was ugly. It got louder and louder. It got screechier and scratchier. Suddenly it stopped . . .

"Where is my Minister of Exact Numbers?" screeched Pharaoh. The Minister appeared. "Tell them, Minister long and thin! Tell them what it means to win! Tell them how many Cross-Over babies have died," screeched the King.

The Minister's face looked gray and tattered, like an old newspaper. He took a piece of paper from his pocket, muttered, "Five thousand seven hundred and forty-six," and disappeared again.

The King glared at Shifra and Pu'ah. He snarled and he snickered, he snickered and snarled: "Did you think you were the only way, when I had to do some killing? A King has many hirelings when there comes a need for killing."

Shifra and Pu'ah took a deep breath in. And out. In again. And out again: "Yyyy-hhhh-wwww-hhhh." Silently they stepped backward into the doorway of Pharaoh's Throne Room, backward and backward until they stood outside the palace door.

* * *

Shifra cried. Pu'ah sighed. Shifra shook. Pu'ah patted her.

Together they walked down the hill and across the meadow to the great wide river at the bottom.

They sat at the edge of the water, watching it murmur and sob. Finally Shifra said, "So the babies are dying anyway. We must do more to save them. What can we do?"

"Talk to the women," said Shifra. "Women understand water. And wells and tears, and milk, and the waters of birth, and the waters of blood. The mothers. The girls. The midwives. The sisters. Not just the Cross-Over women. Even Pharaoh has a daughter. She will not like this business of murdering babies. And there will be others. We two are not enough. But with all of us women together — we can stop that King."

Pu'ah was quiet for a long time. Then she whispered, "What about the men? Only women are people of water; but both women and men are people of air. Of breath. Of wind. The King is killing the boys; it is really the men who are threatened. Why don't we talk with the men?"

Shifra shrugged. Shifra snorted. "Men?" she said. "The King is a man! It is harder for men to wait . . . firmly," she said. "They are not used to giving birth. They are not used to knowing when the time is ripe to act — and when the time is unripe. When it is unripe they are afraid it will never be ripe. So they stay quiet out of fear, not out of waiting. And when they cannot stand waiting any longer, they explode. They force the time, instead of growing ready for the birth. So they use a knife to fight back, to make the birth happen."

But Pu'ah persisted. "The King is a man, but only one man," she said. "The King has forgotten to breathe. But there are men who recall how to breathe. When my father held me close at his chest he would breathe — and his chest would rise and fall. He knew about rising and falling, he knew about holding me close, he knew about air and breath.

"We must gather the Breath of all Life. I will not abandon the men! They must learn to birth with their wives, they must learn how to grow and grow until it is time to birth without killing.

"And then they must teach the women — that even the knife can be used for life. The knife must cut the cord, the knife must hallow the next generation."

So they went to the women and men. They talked to the midwives, the fathers and mothers. They talked to the sisters and brothers:

"We are no longer Cross-Over people, for others will join us. We are a new people, we are just being born. We must have a new name. We must be the Pass-Over people, so that death will pass over our houses."

They met with shepherds and teachers. They met with the King's youngest daughter. They met with a family of dreamers.

They talked, and they laughed, and they cried, and they argued. They sang, they whispered, they waited, they grew.

Some of the women said "Yes" and some of the women said "No." Some of the men said "No" and some of the men said "Yes."

Most of the Cross-over people said "Yes", but some of the Cross-over people said "No." Most of the home folks said "No," but some of the home folks said "Yes." A few of the rich said "Yes", and some of the poor said "No."

So Shifra and Pu'ah chose from the people they met with, and said: "When the moon is round and full, it is time for us to give birth. That night we will meet at the river."

* * *

So the moon began to swell and the people began to stir. On the night when the moon was full, the people made a circle at the river. The moon was round in the sky, and the people were round on the earth.

Shifra sat in the circle, and Pu'ah sat across from her in the circle. The two of them said together: "When a mother is ready to give birth, there must always be one man and one woman with her. The men must learn to give birth, the women must learn to cut the cord. You must go to the bank of the river, and you must sing to the water."

Then Pu'ah nodded to Shifra, and Shifra sang this song: "You are the water of drowning, and You are the water of birthing. Today you must give birth to life. Today you make peace with our children.

"And then you must make the sounds of the water: Sh-sh-sh L-l-l-l- Ommmm."

Then Shifra nodded to Pu'ah, and Pu'ah chanted this chant: "You must say to the air:
"You are the breath
"Of the world.
"Our babies are born into you.
"You must be borne
"Within them.
"And then you must make
The sound of the breath: Yyyy-hhhh-wwww-hhhh."

Pu'ah paused. Then she looked around the circle. "Let us share our dreams," she said. "Dream new!"

One mother put her hand on her belly: "I dream that my child will lead us all — lead us to Pass Over the desert."

One father put his hand on his knife . . . "I dream that my child will teach us all — teach us how the knife can make holy, not dead."

A brother put his hand in the river: "I dream that my sister will dance through the water to freedom."

A sister put her hand on the thorns of a thornbush: "I dream that my brother will see light in these thorns, and give light to us all in our thorniest tangles."

Shifra called out to the princess, the King's youngest daughter.

And the princess said, "My language is different from yours, my words are different from yours. There is only one thing we share. It is breathing. Breathing comes first, before all words. Breathing comes last, when words are done. Breathing comes meanwhile; a breath is the word that includes all words.

"Our children will teach us to share our breath with each other, to share the Breath of Life."

And all the people said together:

"This Breath of Life will make death pass over us all.

"This Breath of Life will make us the Pass-Over people.

"This Breath of Life will become our King — and we will have no King.

"This Breath of Life will bring us out of slavery."

And all of them rose to go back to their houses, to give birth to the Pass-Over people.

* * *

When the moon was high in the sky, the people began to move.

From cities and farms, from palaces and shacks, came a great stream of people, a river of people.

From cities and farms, from palaces and shacks, came groans and shouts, a rushing breath like women panting to give birth.

The earth trembled, the houses shook, the people left.

They sang and they danced.

They blew breath into the horns of rams and goats, and the breath came forth as wails and shrieks of music.

They banged on drums and bells, and the blows came forth as rings and booms of music.

They plucked on strings and puffed on flutes, and all the sounds came forth as tunes of music.

"The world is upside-down!" they sang, and then turned somersaults.

And when they came to the edge of a blood-red sea, the wind arose.

"Yyyy-hhhh-wwww-hhhh, Yyyy-hhhh-wwww-hhhh, Yyyy-hhhh-wwwwhhhh, Yyyy-hhhh-wwww-hhhh," the wind breathed in and out.

The wind pushed and the waters rose, the wind pushed and the waters rose, the wind pushed — and the waters broke.

And the people danced across the sea.

On the other side, the people began to breathe together, making the sound of the wind. "We will never forget the sound of this wind, this breath of life," they said;

"Yyyy-hhhh-wwww-hhhh, Yyyy-hhhh-wwww-hhhh, Yyyy-hhhh-wwww-hhhh, Yyyy-hhhh-wwww-hhhh."

# Part Three
# Tales of Torah

# When the Fire Spoke

oshe chased after the skipping, dancing lamb just as it disappeared around the mountain-side; tripped, cut his knee, and lost one sandal in a bramble patch.

As he rose to hobble up the path, muttering at the bad luck of the morning, he saw another patch of brambles — burning. Yelling "Oh my God!" he dashed to clear a firebreak so that the flames would not spread to the other dry thorn bushes on the mountain. His other sandal clattered unheeded off the path as he approached the burning bush.

He looked into the fire, tongues of flame rising and retreating, thorns popping as they burned. Suddenly the flames burst across the entire tracery of twigs, replaced their black-green with bright orange, flecks of gold and glowing red. What had been a bush afire became a bush of flame.

Time stopped. Moshe gazed. The bush burned, blazed, glowed, changed without changing.

"Who am I?" Moshe said. "And who are you?"

The bush burned, blazed, glowed, changed without changing.

"You. Me. Burning. Burning with shame, my throat burning that I left my people. Burning with anger, my heart burning at their suffering. Eyes burning, burning with a vision for their happiness.

"My God, burning.

"Who are you?"

"I? I! The God of your fathers. Of Amram your father, Jacob your grandfather, Isaac and Abraham their fathers."

"But I said this to them! Yes, before I ran away, I said exactly this to them. When they asked who had sent me to keep them from killing each other, who had put me in authority over them, I told them the God of our fathers had sent me.

"They laughed. They slapped their knees and laughed at me. 'The God of our fathers!' they said. "Where was He when our fathers knelt to Pharaoh? This God we know, this God we knew, this God we have always known. No hero. At best He hates us, at worst He forgets us.

"And the women — much worse. They clicked their teeth at me: 'You men! This God of your fathers is useless to us. Will your freedom come from Him? It comes from us! Your mothers and midwives gave you birth when Pharaoh said to kill you. Your sisters drew you from the river, to make it birthing instead of drowning waters. This God of your *fathers* — what has He ever said to us? At worst He excludes us, at best He ignores us. We must have a new birth of freedom, and no father-god knows how to give birth."

Moshe watched the bush of flame blow sideways, like a shrug. Heard, muttered, "All right. Tell them it is the God of their fathers *and* mothers — Sarah, Rebekah, Rachel, and Leah as well. Then the men will know something new is happening, and so will the women."

Moshe turned pale. "Can't do. *Won't* do. Won't even mention it. Once I do that, they will argue day and night. Some of the men will be angry. Some of the women won't think it's enough: I'll never hear the end of it. As for freedom — forget it."

For an instant the flames roared up like a furnace, and the tongues of flame roared words: "Some day, I will teach such a lesson! . . . Someday. All right. I'll wait. *Some*day there will be women who are willing to insist. And meanwhile . . ."

The flames grew quiet. For many many minutes, Moshe stood in silence, trembling.

Then the flames began to rattle. No, not quite a rattle. A cough? A chuckle? Could it be, a chuckle? Yes, a chuckle, and then: "Tell them, I was what I was, I am what I am, but I will be who I will be. Yes, I will be who I will be. *And so will they.*     Ehyeh asher ehyeh
asher ehyeh asher

ehyeh asher ehyeh
asher ehyeh asher . . ."
The flaming bush became a spiral of fire.

"I who was once the God of your fathers, I learn from mothers how to give birth. I learn and you learn, you learn and I learn; I bear and you are born, you bear and I am born. We will become who we will become.

Ehyeh asher ehyeh
asher ehyeh asher . . ."

Moshe found his arms inscribing in the air before his chest a spiral, in rhythm with the flames and the words the flames were chanting.

"They were slaves, but they can become free people. They were a tiny clump of cells, nestled in a nurturing womb — but they can grow to birth size, and the birth pangs will seize Mother Egypt if Pharaoh tries to block their birthing. They can become who they will become.

"I speak to the women as well. When the midwives heard me, I spoke not from a bush but through a baby. I appeared in every mother's face, I was heard in every baby's cry. How else did they know they must disobey Pharaoh?

"And the women know my Name, as well. My secret Names.

"To Abraham I thundered that El Shaddai meant God-of-the-Mountains, All-Powerful; but to Sarah I whispered that it meant God-of-the-Breast, All-Nourishing.

"And now, my Name can be neither Hebrew nor

Egyptian, for both peoples must come to know me in both tongues. Some of the midwives were Israelite and some were Egyptian; they worked together for life. Miriam is an Israelite, and Pharaoh's daughter, Bat-yah, is Egyptian; they worked together for life.

"So what can be my Name for them both to understand? Only the word that is beneath all words, the word that is beyond all words, the word that is within all words, the word that holds all words within it. The word that is not shaped by human hands, or tongue, or lips — but comes from outward in, from inward out. A breath. *Only a breath.*

"My name is YHWH. Do not put in a vowel, Moshe! Do not try to call me Yahweh; not Jehovah; not Adonai, or Lord, or even Eternal. Just Yyyyhhhhwwwwhhhh, a breathing.

"I am the Breath of Life, and the Breath of Life is what will set you free. Teach them that if they learn my Name is just a Breathing, they will be able to reach across all tongues and boundaries, to pass over them all for birth, and life, and freedom."

Next to Moshe, a lamb tumbled and bahhhhed, licked Moshe's naked feet. Time began to flow again. The fire shook and vanished. The bramble bush was gone. Ashes trembled in the wind.

# The Seven Who Danced in Paradise

The moon glowed round and full in the mid-summer month of Av. Many of the young women of Israel had chosen husbands on the afternoon before; had danced in the fields to celebrate their choices. Now, under trees across the land, bright canopies of color were unfurled to house the marriage ceremonies.

Imma Shalom came to the dancing with her young friend B'ruriah — young enough to be her daughter. Their two husbands, Eliezer and Me'ir, had gone to the far north to settle a law case. The two women were members of a Torah-study group that was unique in all the land, for in it men and women learned together.

Imma Shalom had grown up in a household of

Sanhedrin presidents. Herself a gem of wisdom in the learning and teaching of the Torah, she cared passionately about applying Torah to help the poor and the despairing.

"Too many of our rabbis groan over Torah and laugh at the poor," she said. "I needed a husband who would laugh with me when we studied Torah, and cry with me when we saw beggars on the street. When Eliezer and I turn an ancient text upon its head to find new meaning — that is funny. When we do it to meet the needs of our troubled people — that is serious."

Since she mothered the community for the sake of peace and harmony, the people called her Imma Shalom — Mother Peace. And then they added a wry and loving proverb — "Imma Shalom, Bat Eysh. Mother of Peace, Daughter of Fire." For she was no demure or placid lady, but a bold and fiery woman.

Tonight, indeed, as she celebrated the marriage of a couple even younger than B'ruriah and Me'ir, Imma Shalom was dancing like a storm of fire. She relished dancing with the friends she knew and loved, whirling to the tunes they knew and loved. She looked around her: Yes, all the others of their study band of six were dancing near her: gentle B'ruriah, who showed deep wisdom in her loving knowledge of the Torah; awkward Akiba, who was so deft with language; the dour Elisha ben Abuyah; and the two tall Shimons — ben Zoma and ben Azzai. B'ruriah had joked again and again that it took all four men to keep up with the Torah-learning of Imma Shalom and herself.

Content, Imma Shalom leaned into the music that she knew. But as the night grew darker and the whirling deeper, a woman she had never seen before raised up a pair of timbrels and began to chant a melody that she had never heard. The words, she recognized:
"Kamti ani
lifto'akh l'dodi.
I will open to you, my beloved;
will you open, open to me?"

And she began to chant them with the singer. As her eyes closed and she moved deeper and deeper into the chant, the words themselves began to be her world. After what could have been a moment or an hour, the melody changed, the words changed:
"Your breasts will be tender
as clusters of grapes,"
and then, after a still deeper immersion in the chanting, she dimly heard it change again:
"His belly smooth as ivory,
 bright with gems,"

And then the three different chants became a round, spinning from one melody to the next, woven in a spiral with each other. Imma Shalom thought one last ordered thinking: "I have heard these words before, but never with this music. — What is it? — Ahh! From the Song of Songs that lovers sing when they make love with each other."

She gave herself entirely to the music, letting herself whirl into a dance that wove its path among the wedding guests as the words of the Song wove in and out of the melodies.

As Imma Shalom's body whirled in the dancing, the thoughts whirled in her head. Whirling and swirling, she lost and found herself. Within her and around her danced the words and music. The words became visible, the melodies turned to visions. Within her and around her danced juicy figs and musky apple blossoms, eyes bathed in milk and cooing turtle-doves, women and men whose hair as black as goats wound down the slopes of their own bodies.

Minutes, or hours, or weeks later, Imma Shalom looked around again, Dancing with her in the circle she saw the five beloved others of her Torah circle. The other guests had vanished. Still with them was one other face and body: the nameless singer whose chanting had engulfed her. Whose very face was whirling as she watched: now Miriam, now Ruth, now D'vorah and Tzipporah, now Batya and Batsheva, Tiferet and Tamar.

As Imma Shalom and her six companions danced, the trees themselves began to join the spirals of their joy. A brook gurgled its way into the music, a breeze whistled through a mountain pass. Tossing back her hair to laugh as the seven made an intricate twining with the earthy life around them, Imma Shalom touched hands with Ben Azzai. "Shimon," she called, "What think you of this Garden?"

"Every healing deed is a path into more healing," he said, "and every shattering deed a path toward shattering. But here I see no paths, no shattering, no healing. Here I see only a wholeness past believing. This is the Garden of Delight, of Paradise. Seeing this is all I need to see, living here is all I need to live, leaving here would be more death than dying." He smiled, and died.

The spiral dancing of the six continued. Imma Shalom touched the hand of Ben Zoma. "Dear Shimon," she said, "Don't leave me. What think you of this Garden?"

"It makes no sense to me," he said. "I have studied the Torah of our words and lives, and I have come to learn from paradox. Ask me who are wise, and I will tell you: Not those who teach all people, but those who are so open as to learn from everyone. Ask me who are powerful, and I will tell you: Not those whose armies can assert their will on others, but those who have the power to control their urges.

"So I have learned the heart of Torah, which is paradox. But Paradise is not a paradox. This Garden is not paradox but harmony. This Garden is a Truth, but not a Torah. The Torah is a Truth, but not a Garden. I cannot grasp it, my mind is torn in two." And he began to babble, lost at last in a paradox he could not fathom.

The music slowed, the chant grew quieter, Imma Shalom slowly found herself once more in the rooms where they were dancing. All the guests had left except the six others she had seen as the chant became a vision. "This was somewhere between a dream and prophecy!" she said. "Were the rest of you also on this journey with me?"

Four of the others nodded. But Ben Azzai's death, she saw, was not a dream. On his face remained a smile so deep, so genuine, so good-humored, that she could not find it in her heart to mourn him. "Blessed is the True Judge, truly!" she murmured, though she heard Elisha snort and grunt instead of saying "Amen."

And when she turned to see why Ben Zoma had not answered, she saw he was outside himself, beyond himself; he could not answer.

"B'ruriah, Akiba, Elisha, and you Nameless One — I need to talk with all of you," she said. "This was the strangest evening I have lived through. Will you come home to talk with me?"

Akiba hesitated. "One of us has died, and one seems to be mad. I need to rest, to immerse myself in the sacred waters, to meditate. I do not think that I could bear to talk."

Imma Shalom nodded. "Will you meet with me one month from now, at the full moon of Elul?"

She turned to the woman who had sung so sweetly. "You helped invoke this Garden Paradise for us. What is your name?"

The woman smiled. "Why do you ask my name? Best ask your own. Once you have danced in the Garden Paradise, what is the name that beckons you?"

They all agreed to meet at the next full moon, and each one left for home.

But even before they could gather again, their night of dancing in the Garden was making waves and changes in the country.

First, Elisha ben Abuyah held a public seminar. He sent out word ahead of time that it would be his most important teaching. So all the most learned of the rabbis came, even the ones he had brusquely bested in debates on Torah. Even the politicians he had sneered at came. And all the social climbers who loved to be present when "important" things were happening. And all the local students of Greek philosophy, with whom Elisha had often shared a cup of ouzo.

Elisha stood and smiled, took off his t'fillin, and tossed them at the crowd. They gasped.

"The Greeks are right," he said. "There is no Judge or Justice in the world. The world is beauty, and at its heart is terror. I hear the leopard roar and leap upon the lamb. Its roar is full of beauty and the curve of the leap itself is full of beauty. I shake with terror at the strength and danger of the roar and the leap, but in my very terror is the purity of beauty.

"Then I touch the lamb's soft wool, and I dip my fingers in the redness of its blood. The wool and blood are also full of beauty. Yet most beautiful of all is most terrible of all: the lion devours the lamb. Those are their roles in the great drama of the universe. If they lay down together, or if the red blood turned white as wool, as our silly Prophet imagines — the great drama would lose its terror and its beauty.

"And I see the blood rise in men and women as their passion swells. I see their bodies quiver, I hear them groan like glorious animals. This too is full of beauty. But there is no Justice in it, and any judge who fences it around with rules and statutes destroys its terror and its beauty.

"Forget this Torah and its talk of Justice. Compared to the love songs that are sung in bawdy-houses, the ancient Torah is an empty puff of wind."

Then he sat down. Or he tried to. But the crowd was shrieking, wailing, and a dozen of the Greeks had to lock their arms in a circle around him, to get him out before his own red blood could make a terrible beauty on the sand.

By the next day, the rabbis had rubbed out his name from dozens of Torah teachings in hundreds of parchments. They decided to preserve the teachings themselves, since they could see that there was wisdom in them. But where Elisha's name had been, they wrote in the scarred and empty spaces of the parchment the name Akher — "the Other One."

Meanwhile, reports began to spread that a singer whom no one had ever heard before was appearing in taverns and dance-halls, on the public greens and commons and in the market-places, where the women gathered at the edges of streams to wash their clothing and at the edges of the forests where lovers liked to walk. She was singing the well-known verses of the Song of Songs, but with new melodies that were bewitching. Often she would chant a line or two for hours, and the people — some said — were being driven mad by the music. Cries arose to outlaw the public singing of her chants, or even the very verses of the Song of Songs.

In the midst of all this uproar, sweet and gentle B'ruriah called together the brightest of her students — men and women. Never before had she taught them together. For though she herself had studied as Imma Shalom's protege in the six-fold group with Akiba and the other men, she had till now felt herself too young to lead a group of her own that would challenge the custom of the rabbis.

When her students gathered, they looked at each other shyly, uncertain, ready to flee like deer into the wooded hills. But B'ruriah calmed them, saying she had realized that there would be deeper Torah if they learned together.

"And deepest of all Torah," she said, "is the Song of Songs." Her students gasped. "A woman wrote most of these poems," she said, "and a woman wove them together in this Song. A woman brought them new life through her chanting; now a woman must teach them as Torah." They gasped again. One young man, his voice shaking, said, "But teacher, our rabbis have not even said that these songs are touched with the Holy Spirit. This very night, they are being sung in dance-halls and bath-houses. You say they are the deepest Torah? How do you know?"

"I have lived in the Song, and I know," said B'ruriah.

"This is Torah, the flowing face of Torah. There is a kind of Torah that says, 'Until what time can we do this or that?' That is the Torah the men are always teaching. But here in this Garden, time is much more flowing. 'Do not rouse love until . . . it has its pleasure.'

"When Ruth sang to Boaz on the threshing-floor and took the tunic from his body, these songs are what she sang. She taught us: May those who stoop and sweat to reap the harvest turn to share the kisses of their mouths. When Tamar sang to Judah in the tent to which she brought him beside the road to Timnah, these are the songs she sang him. She taught us: Sing them in the wine-halls to sweeten loneliness, sing them to mystics and to bawdy troubadours, sing them where men dance with men and women with women, and where men and women dance together. Sing them where the bee buzzes and the redwood rustles. Dance them in the most cloistered regal bedrooms of our people.

"Where the men have always taught the God of clock and calendar, we women know the blood of passion flows from our bodies whenever our bodies wish. The men can barely understand this Garden; so we women must teach it to our people. From now on, I will study only the Torah of this Song, and I will do that only with all of you together — men and women."

Within a week, rumors had spread all across the land that B'ruriah had turned the House of Study into a home for lechery and license. "She is sleeping with her own students," some were whispering.

By the time the Sanhedrin met to hear witnesses about the reappearance of the moon for Elul, the land was full of tumult. At the edges of the forests, women were barring the shepherds from their usual pathways, warning that when their flocks ate all the saplings the mountains were left bare to fierce erosion. In Torah-study sessions, those who had always been silent were disagreeing with their teachers. In the market-places, the poor were insisting that the prices of necessities must be cut.

When the Sanhedrin convened, its president was Gam'liel, Imma Shalom's brother, an arrogant man notorious for impatience toward many of the rabbis. Once again he snapped at a well-beloved rabbi, ordered him to stay standing through the whole assembly as a punishment for disagreeing with Gam'liel.

But this time the other rabbis began to shout: "Resign, resign!" until Gam'liel was unable to make himself heard. Finally he left the chair. The Sanhedrin elected a new president. The members invited several hundred students who for years Gam'liel had kept in limbo at the door of the yeshiva to become full members. And they took up a question that had been long postponed, but now was on the lips of all the people: was the Song of Songs to be considered Holy Writ?

The debate was hot. Many argued that no songbook full of erotic wine-hall verses could be sacred. Others pointed out that the Name of God appeared nowhere in the poems: How could they be praise to the Holy One? But others recalled that the wise King Solomon, builder of the Holy Temple, was reputed to have written them. "Maybe when he was sixteen years old and not so wise!" called out one rabbi.

Then Akiba rose to speak. "My learned, worthy brothers," he said, "I myself have lived within the Garden of this Song." The rebellious Sanhedrin hushed.

"Yes, I lived and danced there. But I was not dancing with another mortal, man or woman. These poems are the dance of love between our people and the Holy One of Being. Every kiss is a moment of connection from God to Israel, from Israel to God. Every embrace brings us deeper into union with our Holy One Above. When the woman in these poems searches for her Lover Who is hard to find, we hear ourselves, yearning for the God Who appears and vanishes.

"Of course it was Solomon, builder of our Temple, who wrote these poems. For now that the House of God has been destroyed, the Song of Songs remains for us the Holy of Holies at the heart of our living Temple.

"Let every generation chant these poems at the time of Pesach, the Festival of Freedom. For that is when our God called us to venture into a wilderness, to seek the One Who always vanishes upon the fragrant mountain.

There we became betrothed to our Creator, waiting for the chuppah of the cloud at Sinai; and this is the dance of our betrothal."

Many of the rabbis called "*Keyn yehi ratzon* — May it be God's will!" But a sturdy voice rose above the refrain: "If you are right, Brother Akiba, then this sacred teaching must not be dirtied in the markets and wine-halls of our nation, as if it were a ditty of whores and vagabonds! And it must not be studied where young men and women may think it something other than an allegory."

So the Sanhedrin voted that the Song of Songs had been touched by the Holy Spirit, that at its head should be added the title, "The Song of Songs, which is by Solomon," and that it must no longer be sung in wine-halls or market-places, or anywhere at all except synagogues and houses of Torah-study where men alone would learn its higher meaning.

Two weeks later, when the full moon of Elul rose, B'ruriah appeared at Imma Shalom's house. They shared their news of what was happening: Elisha's heresy; Ben Zoma still babbling; the nameless singer, vanished; the Sanhedrin's vote. The slanders that were being spoken of B'ruriah.

As they were talking, a messenger arrived. He carried a letter from Akiba:

"Dear Imma Shalom, I know that when we danced in the Garden it seemed as if the rivers of Eden were beneath us and around us, that all reality had turned to open flow. I remember seeing waves of depth that invited us to enter and immerse ourselves as if in waves of ocean.

"But do not mistake the appearance of waves for the reality of flow. These waves were written not in water but in marble — a hard, unyielding stone. A stone deep in meaning, a stone that beckons us to see beneath its surface hidden layers of new beauty, but still stone, rigid stone . The world still needs solidity and structure.

"If you try to dive into what look like the waters of the Garden Paradise, I am frightened that you will be crushed by this unyielding stone."

B'ruriah sighed. "So," she said, "Even Akiba is afraid to come, to join with us. He took one step, he persuaded the Sanhedrin to approve the Song, but he has taken our fierce and flowing dancing in the Garden and encased it in a box of stone. He thinks he is protecting it, but I think he is burying what we found.

"And I have not been able to keep teaching what we learned. The rumors about me have frightened my students away. Some of them still come to study with me, but only secretly, only one at a time. A man one afternoon, a woman next morning. In the long run, that will simply make the slanders worse.

"Me'ir believes in me, he scoffs at all the rumors, he holds me close when I tell him the story of the Garden, but he says there is nothing he can do.

"And me — what am I to do? How can I abandon

the joy we felt a month ago?" And she began to sob on Imma Shalom's shoulder.

They cried together. Then Imma Shalom took B'ruriah's hands and looked into her eyes. "Sweet B'ruriah," she said. "You are right. But Akiba is still a partner in our dance. He is burying the Garden, but not in death: he is sowing, as a gardener sows the seed. This notion that the Song is just an allegory is like a tough shell around the tender seed. We are still living in a kind of wintertime; too chilly for our dancing naked in the sun.

"When the sun warms the bodies of our dancing great-granddaughters, the seed will grow and burst the shell apart.

"Wait, I see it, what a joke! — I see, I see, the men themselves, all unawares, will water it toward growing!

"They think this shell — the allegory — is the seed itself. So they will suck on the shell, keep chewing on it, until the shell softens and the seed within turns juicy.

"And then! — The winter is over and gone, the rains have watered the seed, the song of the dove and the dance will be heard in the land.

"And then there will appear not just one bewitched enchanter like our nameless seventh partner, but six hundred thousand swirling dancers who know that every whirling thigh is God.

"Then earth and earthling will dance in joy together; from every breathing human and every breathing tree will flower fragrant growing!"

# The Oven that Coiled
# like a Snake

n a warm spring evening in the town of
Yavneh, dinner had just begun in the home of
Imma Shalom and her husband Eliezer ben
Hyrcanus.

Now Imma Shalom was, as her name said, "Mother
Peace." When people came to her with arguments to settle, she would often say, "In my parents' house I learned
the Torah that 'Both these words and those words are
words of the Living God.' But this is not enough. For if
God is One, these words must somehow mean one thing.
Let us learn the wisdom of this Unity." So she would gently show how two different ways of understanding Torah
could be brought into harmony.

Tonight she brought a loaf of new-baked spicy bread

to the dinner table. "This comes from an oven I have just invented," she said. "Many women have complained to me that it is too easy for their fired-clay ovens to become taboo. Then they must be thrown out and a new oven must be bought. What a senseless waste, a terrible burden for the people! Especially for the women."

"So I have been studying all week the Torah of taboo. We know, of course," she smiled at her husband, "that if an oven is not really one vessel but many different parts, Torah teaches it cannot become taboo. So I have been working to invent an oven that would not be one vessel — and yet would get hot enough to bake the bread.

"So first let us see if the bread is good to eat, and if it is I will explain my oven."

So they took off their wedding rings and said the blessing for the washing of their hands. They washed and dried together, they said the blessing for the bread, and then gently and lovingly each put the wedding ring back upon the other's finger: "*Harei aht . . .*" said Eliezer; "*Harei attah . . .*" said Imma Shalom, as they repeated the commitment of their marriage. And finally they fed each other a morsel of the warm and fragrant bread.

"Wonderful!" said Eliezer. "Your oven makes good bread. Now — what makes you think it cannot become taboo?"

"My oven is something like a barrel, made of clay and sand instead of wood and iron. I began by laying a circle of clay brick," said Imma Shalom. "and then I laid dry sand upon the brick. A coil of brick, a layer of sand; a coil of brick, a layer of sand. The brick is dark, the sand is light; the oven looked from outside like a snake, coiled on itself, ready to spring. So I named it the Oven of Akhnai, the Serpentine Oven.

"Then I put a thick coat of mud around the whole thing, to hold the heat. But no ring of brick is connected to the one above it or below, and so the whole oven is a 'no-thing,' I do not see how any taboo can apply."

Eliezer smiled. "Amazing! You have become a mason beyond masons, a baker beyond bakers. For a mason mixes clay with water; a baker mixes flour and water; but you have mixed the waters of Torah with masonry and bakery, to make a more nourishing Household of Israel!"

Imma Shalom quirked an eyebrow. "Yet you sit in the Sanhedrin, and I do not. — Indeed, though my brother Gam'liel and I learned Torah together in our parents' house, he chairs the Sanhedrin; but I cannot even attend, since you men will not allow women. Will you make sure that the rabbis approve this oven of mine? If you have trouble, let me know; I will talk with my brother. Since he heads the Sanhedrin, let him be of some use!"

Next day, the Sanhedrin convened in the center of Yavneh. Eliezer invited the sages to come look at Imma Shalom's oven. He explained its construction and removed one slice of mud so that they could see the snake-like coils.

"Nevertheless," said Rabban Gam'liel, "although my

sister is so learned," — and his eyebrow quirked just like his sister's — "she has forgotten one important question: How will it seem to those who are not so learned? Indeed, very few men and almost no women are as learned as she. Most of them will look at this oven and think it is 'one thing.' If we do not rule that it is susceptible to taboo, they will think all ovens are free from taboo."

"But wait," said Eliezer, "that makes no sense. She invented this oven exactly to prevent taboo. All over the Land of Israel, if women hear about this oven they will get rid of their old ones and build this kind of Serpentine Oven. They *will* know the difference. That's the whole point! And if they don't know, we can just teach more Torah.

"Think what these stoves will mean to our wives and ourselves! Much less trouble, much less expense. And you yourself admit that it meets the Torah's standards."

"Eliezer, you have always let Imma Shalom twist you around her finger the way a Torah reader rolls the Scroll. She was always very clever, but never very wise. I have ruled!" said Gam'liel.

Eliezer looked around at the other sages. They all nodded, twirling their beards.

"You shortsighted fools!" he said. "You are coiling these stupid arguments 'round and 'round the oven like a serpent — even though you know the Torah permits it. You have been away from home so long that you have forgotten what it means to bake and cook; you have even forgotten your wives. Can any of you remember how beautiful they are? Can any of you remember how wise they are? How on earth can I persuade you?

"Ahh — Earth! If you will not listen to Mother Peace, perhaps you will listen to Mother Earth."

And Eliezer walked outside. He gazed at a nearby carob tree. "O Tree," he said, "If the Tree of Life agrees with me, I ask you to rouse yourself and move one hundred cubits."

The roots of the tree groaned, the tree shivered, its fruit rattled as a breeze brushed its branches, and the tree moved one hundred cubits, where its roots crept back into the ground.

The other sages were rooted to the spot, in fear and wonder. "Trees may move, but we budge not!" said Gam'liel, in a cracked and quavering voice.

Eliezer looked around again. A glittering stream, with tiny waterfalls, ran by the house. "O River!" he said; "If the Wellspring of Truth agrees with me, turn backward; run uphill!"

The water curled and gurgled, foamed and turned backward.

The other sages stared and shook. Said Gam'liel, in a cracked and quavering voice, "Rivers may turn, but we do not reverse ourselves!"

Eliezer looked around again — this time at the House of Study nearby. "O Walls!" he said. "If that Motherly One Who weeps at the Western Wall agrees with me, let yourselves fall, and this House of Study shatter like our Holy Temple!"

Sounds like moans and wailing came from the walls, and they began to lean away from their uprightness. But one of the sages rushed forward and called out: "O Walls! If rabbis seek victories in a war of words against each other, what is your part in this?" And the walls fell no further, out of respect to the sages; but they did not straighten, out of respect for Eliezer. So to this very day, it is possible to see the Leaning Walls of Yavneh.

Eliezer looked around once more. Finally he called, "O Heaven! To Mother Earth they will not listen; if I am right, may Heaven speak."

And a sweet and gentle voice, melodic as the river, a Daughter of the One Most High, echoed softly from the hills and valleys: "Why are you students of My Torah troubling my child, my beloved Eliezer? The sacred path of life is always where he leads you."

But Gam'liel whispered, "Heaven may speak, but our voices will not waver. You, Holy God, taught us in the Torah: 'It is not in Heaven. It is in our hearts and mouths, to do.' And you have also taught, 'Lean toward the majority.' The majority has voted; You and Eliezer must acquiesce."

Eliezer's mouth fell open. "You have twisted the teaching out of shape!" he said. "The Torah teaches, 'Do not follow a majority to do evil, nor respond in a law-case so as to lean toward the majority.' You have ripped the last few words from the Scroll, that is all!"

Gam'liel glared at him. "It is in *our* hearts and

mouths, and *we* will do it." He gestured to the sages to leave Eliezer's house, and they marched back to the center of Yavneh. Then they excommunicated Eliezer. And they ordered that every bowl and oven, every pot and pan, must be burnt in fire that Eliezer had ever ruled free from the danger of taboo.

From all across the Land of Israel, the implements of baking were brought to the central square of Yavneh and thrust into the flames. Many of them cracked and shattered in the heat. And from every kitchen in the land arose the wails of women.

As he listened to the crackle of the flames, the cracking of the vessels, and the sobs of the mothers of the land, Rabbi Akiba, who was one of Eliezer's closest friends, turned to the other rabbis. "If the trees and the rivers did Eliezer's bidding when we were still debating," he said, " what will the whole earth do when he is banned? I ask you — let me be the one to tell him, lest Mother Earth destroy us all!" So the Sanhedrin sent Akiba.

Akiba put on clothes of black, ripped a great gash in the cloth above his heart, wrapped himself in a black tallit, and walked to meet Eliezer — just as if he were mourning someone's death. Instead of coming close to embrace Eliezer as he usually did, he stayed two yards away, as was the rule for those who had been banned.

"Akiba! Why is this day different from all other days?" said Eliezer. "My teacher," answered Akiba, "It seems that today your friends must hold themselves apart from you. And also tomorrow . . ."

Eliezer began to weep, tore his own clothing, took off his shoes, and sat upon the earth, as if he too had been bereft of some beloved.

As he fell upon the ground, Mother Earth herself received his sorrow. Throughout the Land of Israel, one-third of the olives fell dry and shriveled from their trees. One-third of the wheat was spoiled by mildew. And one-third of the barley was devoured by locusts. Not only was there a dearth of the oil and flour used for baking, but in every kitchen the women found the dough for bread had suddenly turned rotten in their hands.

Even the sea fell into turmoil. After proclaiming the ban on Eliezer, Gam'liel had left Yavneh for the nearby coastline, and boarded a ship to visit far Tarshish. A great storm crashed against the vessel, until Gam'liel rose to face the ocean. "I see in these storm clouds the face of Eliezer," he cried out. "I taste in this salt spray the tears of Eliezer. O You Who rule the world, it is Your face I honor. Not for the heavy burdens that I bear as president, nor for the weighty reputation of my family, but for Your radiant Face alone have I stepped forward — lest our sisters, mothers, daughters become embattled with us in our houses."

The sea stopped raging, and Gam'liel returned to his home in Yavneh. Eliezer too returned to his home — shattered and humiliated. To his wife "Mother Peace," Imma Shalom, he said: "I failed you and all your sisters. I could not persuade the Sanhedrin to approve your Akhnai Oven, and your own brother led them into banning me."

Imma Shalom looked at Eliezer's suffering, and her own face took on new lines of sadness and a secret worry. Each day, each week, each month as his loneliness stretched on, she came to pray with him as he murmured words to God. Over and over, his proud bearing failed him and he tottered to his knees and touched the earth. Each time, she caught her breath and ran to help him back to his feet. Over and over, when in his agony he all but fell flat on his face to kiss the earth, she lifted him.

But one day, just as Eliezer began his prayers, there was a knock at the door. Turning, she saw a beggar seeking bread. For a moment she turned back to Eliezer, but saw a flash of pain upon the beggar's face. "No, you are right," she murmured, and found a new-baked loaf to hand him.

Coming back to Eliezer, she saw that he had fallen fully on the earth, his face full of tears, in profound prayer. "Arise," she cried out, "you have killed my brother!"

Indeed, only moments later the shofar sounded from the House of the Sanhedrin in Yavneh: Gam'liel had died.

Eliezer, trembling, rose to his feet. "How did you know this?"

"With him," said Imma Shalom, "I learned this teaching at our mother's knee: Since the burning of the Temple and the closing of its gates, all gates of prayer are closed to us but one: the gate of burning tears and deep humiliation. I knew that once you fell from your high station to the lowly earth, if once you let this humiliation sweep fully over you, it would burn through every cautious gate of Heaven and consume whoever had so brought you low.

"I was caught between you, and my brother, and the beggar. How could I turn away from him when he was hungry? How could I turn away from you when you were shattered? How could I turn away from my brother in his danger?"

For many years, among the rabbis and among the women of the land, the story of Imma Shalom, Eliezer, and Gam'liel was told. And then one day, two generations later, Rabbi Nathan on his journeys met Elijah, the prophet who entered Heaven without ever dying.

"Elijah," asked Nathan, "What did God do on that day when the Rabbis spoke out against the Voice of Heaven and put the ban on Eliezer?"

"On that day," said Elijah, "God spoke three times.

"First God wept, saying, 'Oh Eliezer, my beloved Eliezer, my son, my son, beloved Eliezer!'

"And then God smiled and said: 'My children the rabbis have taken My Torah into their own hearts and mouths; my children the rabbis have been victorious over me; my children the rabbis have made me eternal.'

"And finally God's Face shone full of light and glory, and God said, 'My daughter Imma Shalom has learned to mother the world. By my Life, her daughters will one day bring shalom to all the peoples.'"

# Part Four
# Tales of the Temple

# *Jealous Sister, Jealous God*

t was a night of heat: dry, scorching, heat, the parching winds that dry their way across the Roman Sea. No rain, no water, no cooling breeze of life. In this village outside the Imperial City, a circle of people was squatting on the floor, already thirsting — but tonight they could not drink. The oldest spoke:

"Two hundred years ago tonight, our Holy Temple was in flames, and Roman soldiers were driving my own family into slavery.

"Here we are, two hundred years in exile. We should have celebrated a Jubilee four times by now — the year that comes each fifty years, when every family should have returned to the land-holding of its forebears, the year when all slaves should have been freed. But I no longer have any hope of Jubilee; I see no sign of our return to the land of our forebears. Though we are no longer slaves, we are not free. I have no hope that in my lifetime we will see Judea free or the Holy Temple restored.

"What can we do, what else but sit each year in mourning and wail the Prophet Jeremiah's words of lamentation?

"Last night, I dreamed a dream. It is a day like this one: no rain, no water, no cooling breeze of life. Only heat: dry, scorching heat, the parching winds. The flames of the Temple, still visible behind us; before us, the world itself is burning. All I can see is shimmering waves of air, every breath a step into a furnace. Around me my friends are staggering, falling, dying. I try to speak, but my tongue is swollen; only a whisper comes forth. Yet the words burn like a fever in my bones. What my mouth cannot utter, my whole body, my whole being, shouts toward Heaven:

" 'Our father Abraham, awake! I, Jeremiah, I call you to awake! Cast but one glance upon your dying people, and speak to save us.'

"And I realize that I am living in a body that has just seen the first Destruction, a body that is walking, limping, its path toward Babylon. So long ago that I could not until this moment have imagined it outside the pages of a book.

"Above us I feel a stirring. The clouds of smoke and dust thicken and darken on the desert. The clouds become a shape; the flickering thunder, voices.

"'My God!' says Abraham: 'What are You doing? You sent me on a journey; You and I, we made a covenant. You promised that my seed would be as numerous as the sand; I see them trampled as the sand is trampled, I see them thirsty as the sand is thirsty, but on this journey there is only death. You have broken the covenant; restore them to their land, just as You promised!'

"I heard the thunder roar: 'I am a jealous God, and they were whoring after other gods. I will not tolerate this! — Shout no more wails of lamentation in my ears.'

"I heard a silence. And then another voice, thinner, more plaintive: 'Awesome God, I faced You with no fear, ready to give my own life to honor You. Even when my father's knife descended toward my heart, even when the angel's tear scalded my eyes, I did not blink. You laughed with joy to see my faith and courage, and You promised that my people would not suffer this ordeal. You made a covenant with me; but now the knife — Your knife — descends on tens of thousands, and You strike each heart. You have broken the covenant!'

"Again I heard the thunder roar: 'I am a jealous God, and they were whoring after other gods. I will not tolerate this! — Shout no more wails of lamentation in my ears.'

"Silence, and then another voice: 'My God! I wrestled You, and won Your blessing and the covenant of an endless future. For Your sake I walked limping all my life, but here! — Your people have no strength to limp, they are falling dead. The name You gave us You have hollowed out. You have broken Your covenant!'

"And the thunder rolled, the desert shook: 'I am a jealous God, and they were whoring after other gods. I will not tolerate this! — Shout no more wails of lamentation in my ears.'

"And Moses spoke: 'Oh God of freedom, You have broken Your covenant!' And Aaron: 'Oh God of peace, You have broken Your covenant!' And the Torah Herself, "Oh Lover of Torah, I *am* Your covenant, it is me You destroy!"

"And the Holy Letters themselves, the Aleph and Bet, the Gimel and Dalet, spoke in the sounds of themselves: 'With us You shaped worlds that now You destroy; You have broken Your covenant!'

"But the desert shook as the Voice came again and again: 'I am a jealous God, and they were whoring after other gods. I will not tolerate this! — Shout no more wails of lamentation in my ears.'

"Now there was silence, except for the quiet sounds of suffering around me: coughs of the dying, gasps of children, muffled sobs, murmured words of comfort. Out of these whispers rose another voice from Heaven, calm and assured:

"'You are a jealous God? I know, I understand; I was a jealous woman. When my beloved Jacob and I began to plan our marriage, I was afraid my father would play a trick on us. I knew that he would think my older sister Leah should be married before me; I was afraid that he would substitute Leah for me. I was frightened, crazed with jealousy — and so I taught Jacob some secret signals so that he could know whether it was his beloved Rachel or someone else who came to the wedding bed.

"'And then — just moments before the wedding itself, when my father told me that it was Leah who would go to be with Jacob, my heart broke open. I realized how shamed my sister would be, discovered and exposed so cruelly when Jacob tested her. How shattering! So I taught her the signals. My love for my sister overflowed, and my jealousy was washed away.

"'Yes, I was a jealous woman — and You, You are a jealous God? Jealous of what — dead sticks and stones and empty idols? For this you will destroy Your people? I was jealous of my living, breathing sister, and yet I could not bear to hurt and shame her. How dare You!'

"Once more there was a silence. And then the wind shifted. I felt a cooling breeze. Some drops of gentle rain began to fall, and I saw some of the sick around me turn their mouths upward, lick their lips to suck the water in.

"And the Voice came gentle, sad: 'Mother Rachel, for Your sake I will redeem them. Where they are going, I will watch over them. I will help them to turn their lives once more toward Me. And in seventy years, I will return them to their homes.' "

The old man looked around the circle, quirked an eyebrow: "As we all know, from Babylon they did return. And we — what can we learn from Mother Rachel?"

# New Life in the Coffin

t was early summer in the year 70 of the Common Era. The Imperial Roman Army had occupied the whole Land of Israel, and was besieging the Holy Temple. No food or water could enter — but secret water-sources and a ten-year supply of food were keeping the Temple defenders strong.

For some of the defenders, this was not enough. "These Romans are corrupting our Land and our People," they cried out. "What is a Temple with no offerings, no pilgrims? We must drive the Legions out!"

Burning with zeal, they worked out a plan. "Our Jewish brothers think they can outlast the Romans because they have ten years of food in storage. But if we burn the food that the Temple keeps stored away, our brothers will have no alternative. They will have to go on the attack. If we are brave enough, God will come to our aid. If we force God to choose — win everything or lose everything, lose even the Holy House of Your Own choosing! — surely God will take up arms against the enemy."

There were two among the Temple soldiery who urged great care. One said, "Remember when our forebears sent the Holy Ark itself into battle against the Philistines so that God would give us victory — but God laughed and let the Ark be captured?" The other said, "Remember those who laughed at Jeremiah's warnings and shouted scornfully, 'It is God's Holy Temple, it is God's Holy Temple; surely no evil can befall it.' Yet the armies of Babylon descended and destroyed it!"

But the Zealots called the two dissenters to an emergency court-martial, convicted them of treason for "undermining morale," and had them stoned to death on the wall at the edge of the Temple area. Then they pushed their bodies over the wall into the Roman camp, laughing as they pushed: "We can have no dead bodies in the Temple's holy space. Go! — Join the dead gods of these idolators!"

And then the Zealots burned the food.

One of the oldest of the Sanhedrin's holy teachers, Yokhanan ben Zakkai, watched the flames consume the food. "Now it is the food that burns," he muttered; "soon it will be the Temple that burns. Oh, woe. Woe! For this House and all our people!"

A Zealot overheard his wail of woe, and Yokhanan was called before a court-martial. "Why did you say,

'Woe'?" they demanded. Remembering what had happened to the critics, he answered, "I said not 'Woe' but 'Wow!'"

The Zealots freed him, for of him it was prophesied, "Wisdom saves the life of one who has it." Yokhanan explored the Temple area. He found soldiers reduced to eating soup that was made from boiling straw. "With soup made from boiling straw they will defeat the legions of Vespasian?!" he said. "I must get out of this place!"

When he asked for permission to leave, the Zealots refused. "Of course, if you were dead —" they guffawed. "Remember, the dead we throw over the wall!"

"Better pretend death in order to live than — like these fools — pretend life so as to die," thought Yokhanan. So he asked his students to nail him in a coffin and carry him outside the Temple walls.

When his students opened the coffin, word spread that a great teacher had arisen from the dead. So the Roman general Vespasian called for Yokhanan to appear before him.

"Hail, O Emperor!" said Yokhanan.

"Quiet!" said Vespasian. "For I am but a general, and if the Emperor should hear of this, he will have me executed for high treason."

"Nevertheless," said Yokhanan, "Hail, O Emperor!"

So Vespasian threw him in a dungeon.

But three days later, a messenger arrived from Rome. The Emperor had died, and the Senate had elected

Vespasian the new Emperor. He freed Yokhanan from prison, and said to him, "O great magician! Ask of me a gift!"

Said Yokhanan, "I am no magician; I simply know the Torah. It is written, 'Lebanon will be destroyed by a mighty leader.' 'Lebanon' means our Holy Temple, built of the cedars of Lebanon; and no mere general could be called a mighty leader."

"Still," said Vespasian, "magic you do and magic I need. I need a healing; for ever since the news of my election came, my feet are swollen and will not fit my shoes."

"Have a slave come and insult you," said Yokhanan. Vespasian's face turned purple with rage, but he muttered, "You are a great magician," and ordered a slave to call him nasty names until his face turned pale in humiliation. In that moment, his feet returned to normal.

"How did you know this, great magician?"

Said Yokhanan, "I am no magician; I simply know the Torah. It is written, 'Good news swells up the bones; but a broken spirit dries the bones.'"

"Still," said Vespasian, "Magic you do and magic I need. Ask of me a gift."

"Spare our Holy Temple and leave our Holy City," said Yokhanan.

"Did Rome give me the Tenth Legion, send me so far, and make me Emperor to spare your Temple? Ask a different gift!"

"Then give me the village of Yavneh where I can

teach the Holy Torah to young students," said Yokhanan.
"This healing magic that you know?" said Vespasian. "So
be it!"

And so as the Holy Temple went down, through the
wisdom of our teacher Yokhanan the Holy Torah ascended.

# When the Black Ox Bellowed

ne day on a farm far from Jerusalem, a Jew was plowing when his black ox began to bellow. "Wait!" said his neighbor, who was an Arab. "Unyoke your ox and pause in your plowing, for your Holy Temple has been destroyed."

"How do you know this?" asked the Jew.

"I can hear it from the bellow of your ox," he answered.

"I do not understand the meaning when the black ox bellows; but still, my friend, I will take your advice." He unhitched the ox and began to mourn.

Then the ox bellowed again, and the Arab said, "Harness your ox and resume your plowing!"

"And why should I do this?" asked the Jew.

"Because I hear from the bellow of your ox that your Messiah has been born!"

"And what is his name?"

"His name is 'Comforter.'"

"And where does he live?"

"He lives in Bethlehem."

"I do not understand the meaning when the black ox bellows; but still, my friend, I will take your advice." He reharnessed his ox and began to plow.

But that night he told his wife and children, "I must find out whether what the black ox says is true." The next day, he drove the ox to the village market, sold the ox and the plow, and with the money bought a package of velvet baby clothes.

From one city to another, he walked and walked, carrying the velvet baby clothes upon his back. From one region to another, he walked and walked, carrying the velvet baby clothes upon his back.

At each stop upon his journey, he went to the village market. "Is there here a farmer who owns a black ox?" he asked. In every town, there was one black ox. He sought out the owner, and when they met he asked each time, "What news of the Holy Temple?"

"All is well and the offerings are well," said those who owned black oxen.

But when he reached Jerusalem, he did not go to the marketplace. He went to the Holy Temple. But he found it in ruins. When he asked on what day it had been destroyed, he learned it was destroyed on the day his black ox bellowed.

So once more he began to walk, From one city to another, he walked and walked, carrying the velvet baby clothes upon his back. From one region to another, he walked and walked, carrying the velvet baby clothes upon his back. Finally he arrived in Bethlehem.

From one door to another in the town of Bethlehem, he walked and walked, carrying the velvet baby clothes upon his back. At every house where there was a young baby, the mothers bought a suit of baby clothes. But he came to a house where the mother said, "I have a small baby, but I will not buy your clothes."

"Why not?" said the farmer.

"Because a hard fate is in store for my baby. On the day my child was born, our Holy Temple was destroyed."

"Yet for such a baby, born in pain and sorrow, it is necessary to wear velvet clothes! Let us trust in our God YHWH Whose Name is the Breath of Life, Who breathes in and breathes out. Take these velvet suits to clothe your baby, and on the next new moon I will come back to you. Then you can pay me."

So the farmer went away. When he returned at the time of the new moon, he found the house draped in black and the woman in tears.

"What has happened?" he said.

"I dressed my baby in your velvet clothes," the mother said, "and at that moment a great wind roared through our city. A whirlwind came and lifted my child , whirling and whirling the child high in the air. "

"Blessed be the breath of the world Whose Name is the Wind," said the farmer. "As for you, know that your child is safe, hidden away till the day shall come when all can hear the Voice of the Breath of Life. And on that day, your child will bring Comfort to all the earth. For I have learned that your child will be Messiah!"

"How do you know this?" said the weeping mother.

"I know it from four teachings," said the farmer:

"First, the teaching of my old black ox; for when Messiah comes, all earth will know, the animals will speak it. Once again they will be free, and they will tell us.

"Second, the teaching of my friend the Arab. For only when the families of Abraham can hear each other will Messiah come.

"Third, the teaching of the Torah; for it is written, 'Lebanon' — that is, our Holy Temple, built of cedars of Lebanon — 'will be destroyed by a great leader,' and in the next verse it is written, 'And a shoot shall spring forth from the stump of Jesse, a twig from the roots of David's offspring.'

"And fourth, the teaching of the rushing-wind and spirit Who has hidden your child until the time will ripen.

"So come with me and share my children, let them be your comfort until your child shall blossom as our Comforter."

# In the Twinking
# of an Eye

o the hills of Israel where the air is clearest and it is possible to see the furthest —
To the little town of Tz'fat above the Lake Kinneret —

Long ago there came a Hassid, visiting from Vitebsk to see his Rebbe.

Struggling up hills, over cobblestones, through narrow alleyways, the Hassid came panting, shaking, to the door of a pale and quiet synagogue.

So pale, so quiet was this shul that the pastel paintings on the wall and ceiling stood out as though they were in vivid primary colors.

As the Hassid came into the shul, he saw his Rebbe

high on a makeshift ladder, painting a picture on the ceiling above the bimah.

The Hassid blinked, startled to see his Rebbe with a paint brush in his hand.

And then he blinked again. He frowned and tugged at his beard:

"Rebbe, what is this that you are painting here above the bimah? It looks like the Dome that the Children of Ishmael, the ones they call Muslims, have built above the rock where Abraham bound Isaac.

"The giant golden Dome that they have built where stood the Holy Temple. I have just come from Jerusalem . . . It looks . . ." He stopped.

The Rebbe's eyes turned inward. "You know," he said, "Here in Tz'fat we can see and see and see . . . so far! And I have seen . . ." he said, and paused. "I have seen . . ." he said and paused again.

"Looking and seeing, they can be so strange. For example — our sages teach us that when Messiah comes, he will rebuild the Holy Temple in the twinkling of an eye. But often have I wondered: How can this be? Messiah will be extraordinary, yet still a human being merely . . .

"But now! I have seen . . . Well, let me tell you: at the foot of the Western Wall, the Wall where God's Own Presence weeps and hides in exile, I have seen hundreds of thousands of Jews gathered, singing.

"Messiah has come! — and they are singing, dancing, as the Great Day dawns. Women, men, together — I could not believe it! I was not even sure" — he glanced apologetically at his Hassid — "whether Messiah was a wo-  . . . well, forget it.

"I can see from the sun, the heat, it is late afternoon. Yet the crowd are wearing *t'fillin*. So I can see that it is Tisha B'Av, the day of mourning for our beloved Temple. But there are no signs of mourning — except perhaps the way, the wistful way, Messiah reaches out to touch the Wall, to tuck one last petition between the great carved stones.

"I see Messiah speak a sentence to the crowds. I cannot hear the words, but I can see that from this voice there stirs a river. Like water from the ancient stones of the Wall, I see a stream of Jews flow up the stairway that rises to the Temple Mount.

"The river of people pauses on the steps. They cluster 'round a wrinkled, tattered piece of paper, posted above the stairway. I see it is signed by the rabbis of that day. It warns all Jews to go no further, lest by accident they walk — God forbid! — into the space set aside as the Holy of Holies.

"Messiah reads. And laughs. And tears the sign to shreds. The stream of people shudders — higher, higher.

"The crowd cascades from the stairway onto the great stone pavement of the Temple Mount. Their singing turns to the thunder of a great waterfall. They look toward the other end of the Mount — toward the great golden Dome of the Rock where Abraham bound his son for sacrifice.

"Surrounding the Dome are thousands of these children of Ishmael, these Muslims. They are not singing. They are shouting, furious, stubborn. 'Not here!' they shout in unison, 'Not here!'

"'You will not tear down our Holy Mosque to build your Jewish Temple!'

"But I can hear the crowd of Jews — muttering, whispering, 'Right there, yes! — That is the place... No doubt, no doubt, the ancient studies tell us that it is the place.'

"Messiah is quiet. The sea of Jews falls to a murmuring, falls silent. They turn to watch. Messiah looks, gazes, embraces with fond eyes the Holy Space. Messiah's eyes move across the Dome, its golden glow, the greens and blues and ivories of the walls beneath it.

"I hear a whisper from Messiah's lips: 'So beautiful!'

"The Muslims too are silent now. The stillness here, the stillness there — so total that they split the Holy Mount in two.

"Messiah raises one arm, slowly, slowly. The Muslims tense, lift knives and clubs and shake them in the stillness. The Jews tense, ready to leap forward with their picks and shovels.

"Messiah points straight at the Dome.

"The peoples vibrate: two separate phantom ram's horns in the silent air, wailing forth a silent sob to Heaven.

"Messiah speaks quietly into the utter quiet:

'This green, this blue, this gold, this Dome — This is the Holy Temple!'

"I blink.

"For seconds, minutes, there is not a sound.

"Then I hear a Muslim shout, see him raise a knife: 'No! No! You will not steal our Holy Mosque to make your Jewish Temple!

"He throws the knife. It falls far short. No one stirs. The other Muslims turn to look at him. They look with steadfast eyes: no joy, no anger. They just keep looking. He wilts into the crowd; I can no longer see what he is doing.

"Messiah steps forward, one step. Everyone, Jew and Muslim, breathes a breath. One Jew calls out: 'You must not do this. You must not use their dirty place to be our Holy Temple. Tear it down! — We need our own, the prophets teach how wide and tall it is to be. It is not this thing of theirs, this thing of curves and circles.

"He takes a step toward Messiah, lifts an ax to brandish it.

"The man beside him reaches out a hand and takes the ax. Just takes it. There is a murmur, but the murmur dies. The man holds the ax level in both hands, walks out with it into the no-man's-land between the crowds. He lays it on the pavement, backs away.

"There is another time of quiet. Two Muslims reach out from the crowd, toss their knives to land next to the ax. The pause is shorter this time. Then on every side weapons come flying through the air to land beside the ax, beside the knives. There is a pile. Someone walks forward, lights a fire. The pile begins to burn. The flames reach up and up and up — to Heaven.

"So I have seen," the Rebbe said, "Messiah build the Temple in the twinkling of an eye. And that is why I am painting this Dome upon our ceiling."

The visitor took breath again. "And why?" he said. "Why would Messiah do this dreadful thing?"

The Rebbe put his arm around his Hassid's shoulder.

"You still don't see?" he said. "Even here in Tz'fat, you still don't see?

"I think Messiah had four reasons:

"First for the sake of Abraham's two families.

"Second for the sake of the spirals in the Dome.

"Third for the sake of the Rock beneath the Dome.

"And fourth for the sake of the twinkling of an eye."

"And Rebbe — why did the people burn their weapons?"

"For the sake of the burnt offering. It is written that when the Temple is rebuilt, there must be burnt offerings. And it is also written, 'Choose!'

"Choose what? Choose what to burn:

"Each other, and the Temple, yet again?

"Or — the things we use to burn each other with."

"So ..." said the Hassid, "... dear Rebbe — you are saying that the Dome — it really is our Temple?

"Forgive me, Rebbe, but I wonder whether the Temple may be the empty space. The empty space where the offering went up in flames to Heaven.

"The empty space between them, where they burned the weapons — perhaps that is the Temple?

"Ours and theirs?"

The Rebbe turned, astonished, to gaze more deeply into the Hassid's eyes. "I see!" said the Rebbe.

And then together, each with an arm around the other's shoulder, together they walked to where their eyes could look:

Far, far beyond the hills, much farther than the Lake they call Kinneret.

# Sources:
# Once Upon a Time . . .

These stories, of course, have their origins in other stories. (Even stories that emerge from an actual event take richer resonance from how that event echoes other stories.) Indeed, the telling of "sources" is one of the richest forms of storytelling — for every story really begins with a tale about itself:

"Once upon a time, we were . . . *reading* . . . or *watching* . . . or *doing* . . . when this story came to us."

So we will run through the stories of this book in just that way.

\* \* \*

"The Rest of Creation" comes from two times in Arthur's life.

One evening in the summer of 1974, he started to read aloud to his children — then ten and seven years old — a schoolbook with stories of God's Creation of the world. "Booooooooring!" said David and Shoshana. "Think we can do any better?" Arthur asked. "Sure!" they chorused, and together they wrote a set of stories, "Before There Was a Before." Arthur questioned, the kids answered and dictated. He wrote it down, the kids edited, he polished.

In these stories, God started out lonely, became only temporarily a Parent, and grew into a Friend and Coworker. As the World grew more mature, it took a greater and greater part in the Creative process. The Creation according to Buber.

For ten years, the three of them told the stories, wrote the stories, finally found a publisher for the stories. By then David and Shoshana were going their own ways into their adult lives. For Arthur, the very last chapter of *Before There Was a Before* — the chapter of Shabbat, the seventh day, the day of rest — kept swirling in his head.

Not only had he come to see Shabbat as a healing for his own workaholism, but he became convinced that one reason the human race is in such danger of self-destruction is that for five hundred years — the modern era — the human race has not made Shabbat. Not rested from its work, technology, doing, inventing, in order to rest, reflect, rethink, reevaluate — to be.

Shabbat, he realized, is both cosmic and political.

Both what the Universe needs in order to seal its own continuity and creativity, and what human beings need in order to be free. (In the Exodus version of the Ten Commandments, Shabbat is called a remembrance of Creation [Ex. 20: 8-11, echoing Gen. 2: 1-3]; in the Deuteronomy version, it is called a remembrance of liberation from slavery. [Deut. 5: 12-15; see also Ex. 16: 21-30].)

To heal the world, the most important work we can do is *not working* — resting. Our deepest, most serious need — is to be playful! This playful message itself seemed to call for a playful medium: the language of myth and storytelling that adults would hear and kids could understand.

So in 1986, Arthur wrote and *Hadassah* published "The Rest of Creation." The title is of course a pun that, like most Jewish puns, is serious. It addresses the most profound puzzle of Shabbat: Is it about resting from Creation, or is it "the rest of" — the very last and necessary part of — Creation? The pun is also about the process of Arthur's writing on Creation, for this story is "the rest of" *Before There Was A Before*. In both senses.

* * *

"The Return of Captain Noah" is rooted in the story of the Flood, from Gen. 5: 28 to Gen. 9: 28, and especially in two ancient midrashic comments on the story.

One is that Midrash Rabbah (Bereshit Rabbah XXIII: 3, Soncino, p. 194) gives a name to Noah's wife, who is not named in the Torah text itself. The midrash says that she was Na'amah, who is mentioned in Gen. 4:

135

22, and whose name, like Noah's, meant "restfulness, pleasantness."

In the other, the Talmud offers two explanations for an oddity of the Torah tale: After Noah's family entered the Ark, there was a seven-day delay before the great rain began to fall. The Talmud (T. B. Sanhedrin 108b, Soncino, p. 744 ) explains that the righteous Methusaleh had died, and God decreed a pause for the mourning period of *shiva* in the hope that the world would yet repent, and so avert the coming Flood. The Talmud adds that during this pause of seven days, the sun rose in the West and set in the East, thus reversing the process of creation.

For many years Arthur worked with communities of Godwrestlers and Torah-dancers to draw on the Noah story for wisdom about dealing with the danger of nuclear holocaust and environmental disaster. Over and over, in these discussions people would say that if the Torah had taken Noah's wife seriously enough to name her, it would all have been different: she would have insisted not just on a fruitless warning, not just on saving a pair of every species, but on actually preventing the entire Flood, by teaching the human race how to heal the planet.

When Phyllis and Arthur asked themselves how Noah would react to the present world environmental crisis, they drew on this emerging midrash about Na'amah. How would she have used the final seven days of pause and warning? Out of this question came seven stories, one for each of the seven days of Creation, each according to the *S'phirah* of that day. The *S'phirot* are forms through which Kabbalah, Jewish mysticism, describes the emanations of God that generate our reality. In our generation, Reb Zalman Schachter-Shalomi has taught how to see the *S'phirot* infused within each human being's inner life and spirit. He has also pointed out how any *S'phirah* can become a parody of itself if it is not kept in balance with the others, and can thus corrupt and twist the clarity of our spirits.

We have drawn on Reb Zalman's approach to tell the seven stories of the Seven Days in which Noah and Na'amah reverse the decree of destruction and begin the healing of the earth.

\* \* \*

Whenever Phyllis is asked how the story of Hagar and Sarah came to her, she refers people to the process she describes in the story itself: she learned it from her mother.

Why, of all the mother-stories she might have chosen to retell, did Phyllis feel this one so vividly? First, because it galled her that when we meet one of the few women of the Torah who has a name, who speaks with God, the Prophet Sarah is presented and remembered for cruelty to Hagar. Still worse! — the story of Hagar and Sarah appears not just once but twice in the yearly cycle of the Torah reading, repeated so as to imprint their enmity on the people's consciousness.

To Phyllis, this felt intolerable. She felt it was essential to balance this jealous version from the pen of Moses with the oral Torah that arose from communities of women. What a difference it might make for women's lives, if they saw Biblical heroines walking a path of loving collaboration rather than jealous revenge!

\* \* \*

"The Long Narrow Pharaoh and the Pass-Over People" is based on Chapter I of the Book of Exodus, where the midwives Shifra and Pu'ah appear as the first leaders of what became the Exodus from Pharaoh's slavery.

In drawing on the Biblical story of the midwives and the Exodus, we have used the phrase "The long narrow kingdom" as a translation or explanation of Egypt or "Mitz-ra-yim," which in Hebrew literally means "Narrow Place."

The "Cross-Over People" is a translation of "Ivrim, Hebrews," which literally means "those who cross over" and may originally have been a word of contempt for foreigners, like "wetbacks."

As for "the Breath of Life" and its pronunciation "Yyyyhhhhwwwwhhhh," this is based on the Bible's holiest name for God: the Hebrew letters that are equivalent to "YHWH." If you try to pronounce these letters with no vowels and no space in between them, they sound like a breath. This perception first came to Arthur (undoubtedly to other Jews long long before) while he was teaching a class on Martin Buber. See "The Breath of Life," pp. 278-281, in Arthur's book Godwrestling — Round 2 : Ancient Wisdom, Future Paths (Jewish Lights, 1996), for the story of the discovery.

The birthing midrash that runs through this whole version of the story of the Exodus has emerged from women and men as women have become fully involved in making midrash, during this past generation. See the chapter called "Giving Birth to Freedom," also in *Godwrestling — Round 2* for some of the story behind the story.

\* \* \*

The story of the Burning Bush is told in Exodus 3-4. Phyllis and Arthur generated this midrash by exploring what Moses might actually have heard if he had been fully open to the One Who Fills Heaven and Earth, what was impossible for him to hear because of his own social and psychological boundaries, and what he might have heard but refused to repeat because he feared the people would refuse to listen to someone who told the whole truth.

\* \* \*

"The Seven Who Danced in Paradise" is an exploration of the story told in the Talmud (T. B. Chagiga 14b; Soncino, pp. 90-91) about the four rabbis who "entered Pardes." We asked ourselves about the "missing persons" of the story — three women, two of whom are actually among the very few women named as teachers of Torah in the Talmud, and who were living in the same generation as the Pardes Four. Surely these two great women — B'ruriah and Imma Shalom — had not been left behind when their friends went into Pardes! What parts of the story, we asked, were omitted when the women were omitted?

"Pardes" means literally a delightful garden or orchard, metaphorically therefore "Paradise." It also was used symbolically by the rabbis of the Talmud to symbolize the four paths of interpreting Torah represented by the four Hebrew letters PRDS — P 'shat, the plain meaning of the text in its original historical context; Remez, the allegory that the text hints at; D'rash, the interwoven web of meanings that come from searching in the interwoven web of words and letters from several different texts; Sohd, the mystical meaning of the text as it might arise in God's own reading of it. Since for the rabbis the rich process of studying the many levels of Torah was itself a taste of Paradise, they reinterpreted the word itself to symbolize such study.

So this fusion of the Garden, Paradise, a direct mystical experience of the Divine, and the study of Torah led us to imagine that famous trip into Pardes as a journey into the very Garden of the Song of Songs. The connection came also out of the history of the great Rabbi Akiba, who was one of "the Four" who traveled into Pardes; was the great proponent of the Song of Songs when the Sanhedrin came to a vote over whether the Song was to be considered a sacred text; and was also the rabbi who proclaimed that in his day the Mashiach had come, in the person of the guerrilla warrior Bar Kochba. (For these aspects of Akiba's life and the great revolutionary moment when the Sanhedrin overthrew its president and then voted to canonize the Songs of Songs, see

Berakhot 27b-28a, Soncino, pp. 166-170; Chagiga 14b, Soncino, pp. 90-91.)

The Talmud treats B'ruriah with great respect. (See stories about her at Berakhot 10a, Soncino, pp. 51-52; Eruvin 53b-54b, Soncino, p. 374; Pesachim 62b, Soncino, p. 313, among others.) Yet Rashi, more than 500 years later, tells a scurrilous tale in which her husband Rabbi Me'ir tries to trick B'ruriah into being sexually seduced by one of his students, and succeeds. We cannot believe that the Me'ir or the B'ruriah who are described in the Talmud would have behaved this way; so we accepted the challenge of imagining what events might have started such terrible rumors. (See Rashi, commentary on Avodah Zarah 18b.)

Our sense of Imma Shalom's role in the "Pardes" story was shaped by her role in the story of "The Oven that Coiled Like a Snake," which we discuss below. As for the third, unnamed woman in our story — she owes much of her being to Rabbi Shefa Gold, whose new forms of Hebrew chanting and whose extraordinary spiritual leadership have taken us and many Jewish communities into new places of the spirit. And part of our understanding of this third, unnamed, mysterious woman is rooted in our understanding of the Holy Shekhinah.

* * *

The tale of "The Oven that Coiled Like a Snake" is told in the Talmud (T.B. Baba Metzia 59b; Soncino pp. 352-355). Our reworking of the story came in two stages. First we realized that traditional readings of the story emphasize the victorious verbal skills of the rabbis, and God's celebration and approval of those skills; but that the story as a whole also points out that the use of these skills had disastrous consequences. Disasters fell upon the earth, upon Jewish society as a whole, upon the Sanhedrin, and upon both sides of Imma Shalom's family — her husband and her brother.

To us, Imma Shalom seemed the key to the story. Her brother and her husband were opponents in the story; she attempts to pick up the shattered pieces of the family at the end; and in the Talmud's overall structure and placement of this story, her teaching about God's response to the prayers of the humiliated is the story's punch line — its main point.

As we were realizing this, we also realized — especially out of conversations with David Waskow — that one thread of the story is about the tension between the verbal skills of the male rabbis and the domestic communal needs and skills of women, connected perhaps with the rhythms of the earth. So from this perspective as well, it seemed to us that Imma Shalom had played a much more important role in the original events, or in the original story, than the Talmud's version describes. In the Talmud's version, Rabbi Eliezer takes her place. He becomes a kind of surrogate woman, carrying women's earthy, domestic, and communal values against his verbal brethren.

"Why?" we asked. And it seemed to us that in the story as in reality, Imma Shalom had been screened, masked, because as a woman she could not be fully visible. Until the story's very end, Eliezer stands in for her.

So we started work on our version of the story by asking ourselves what else Imma Shalom did in these events, besides picking up the shattered pieces of her family at the end. From that question flowed the story as we tell it.

For evidence of the tension between Imma Shalom and her brother Gam'liel, see T. B. Shabbat 116a-116b, Soncino, p. 571.

\* \* \*

Three of the four "Tales of the Temple" come from Midrash Rabbah on *Eicha* — midrash on the Book of Lamentations, which bewails the Destruction of the Temple by the Babylonians. By writing midrash on *Eicha*, the rabbis addressed the profound issues created in their lives by the Roman Empire's destruction of the Second Temple. The tale of Our Mother Rachel's appeal to God is told in *Eicha* Rabbah Proems XXIV, Soncino, pp. 42-49; the tale of the Bellowing Black Ox in *Eicha* Rabbah on Chapter 1, verse 16, section 51, Soncino, pp. 136-137; and the tale of Yokhanan ben Zakkai in Eicha Rabbah on Chapter I, verses 4-5, section 31, Soncino, pp. 101-105.

\* \* \*

Finally, the tale of the Rebbe and Hassid in Tz'fat and the Mashiach's way of rebuilding the Temple emerged from at least two sources.

One was that in 1969, visiting Tz'fat, Arthur actually saw a synagogue where on the ceiling appeared a painting of the Dome of the Rock, one of the great Muslim mosques on the Temple Mount in Jerusalem.

The other was our struggle both to understand and to reach beyond the mentality that has led to several attempts by Jewish terrorists to blow up the Dome of the Rock, in order to make possible the construction of the Third Temple on its site. How could we both affirm the traditional Jewish yearning for a Messianic renewal of the Sacred Space on the Temple Mount, and reject the violence and the triumphalism that often seems to accompany that yearning? Surely for the true Messiah a rebuilding of the Holy Temple could only happen in an atmosphere of holy Shalom!

As the story evolved over decades of telling, and our understanding of *tikkun* became deeper, two new elements entered our telling of the tale: the reversal of relationships between Rebbe and Hassid, in which the Rebbe begins to learn from his student and follower; and a new conclusion, in which the empty space of Mystery and In-Between becomes the Sacred Space. These are, in a sense, the same teaching about God's unpredictable, mysterious healing of the world. For *tikkun* to happen, we must be open to the healing that comes in unexpected ways and from uncharted places.

In that spirit, we welcome questions, comments, and responses to these stories. We especially encourage all who enjoy these stories to sojourn at Elat Chayyim (99

Mill Hook Road, Accord, NY 12404), the retreat center where we both teach and where we gave birth to many of these tales, and to become members of ALEPH: Alliance for Jewish Renewal, the international network where our lives and stories flow together. (Readers can write us with questions at ALEPH, 7318 Germantown Ave., Philadelphia, PA 19119, and become members by sending $36 to ALEPH at that address.)

May the One Whose Story intertwines all stories teach us to be open to each other's stories, and through connecting them make One in earth and Heaven.

— *Phyllis Ocean Berman*
— *Arthur Ocean Waskow*

# About the Authors

Phyllis Ocean Berman founded (in 1979) and continues to direct the Riverside Language Program, a renowned intensive English-language school for adult immigrants and refugees from all around the world. It is housed in Riverside Church in New York City. Out of that work she co-authored a book of stories of the lives of immigrants, *Getting Into It*.

Berman is the program director of Elat Chayyim, a Jewish retreat center for healing and renewal near Woodstock, New York, where woods, fields, an organic vegetable garden, and a swimming pool are intertwined with prayer, Torah-study, yoga, meditation, and Jewish art and music. She has written on new liturgy (especially for or about women) for the journals *Good Housekeeping*, *Moment*, and *Menorah*, and for the volume *Worlds of Jewish Prayer* (Jason Aronson, 1993). She often leads "chanting services" in the tradition of her teacher Rabbi Shefa Gold and Torah services focused on "blessing aliyot" in the tradition of Reb Zalman Schachter-Shalomi.

She chaired the board of P'nai Or Religious Fellowship for many years, and is now secretary of the board of ALEPH: Alliance for Jewish Renewal. In 1991, Berman was ordained an Eshet Hazon (Woman of Vision) by the Jewish-renewal women's community.

Arthur Ocean Waskow is a Pathfinder of ALEPH: Alliance for Jewish Renewal, and director of The Shalom Center, a division of ALEPH that works to heal and protect the earth. He is a Scholar in Residence at Elat Chayyim, the founder and editor of ALEPH's journal *New Menorah*, and author of *The Freedom Seder* (Micah Press, 1969); *Godwrestling* (Schocken, 1978); *Seasons of Our Joy* (Bantam, 1982; Beacon, 1990); *Down-to-Earth Judaism: Food, Money, Sex, and the Rest of Life* (Morrow, 1995), and *Godwrestling — Round 2 : Ancient Wisdom, Future Paths* (Jewish Lights, 1996), along with many other works of Jewish renewal. The last of these won the Benjamin Franklin Award.

In 1995 he was ordained a rabbi by a committee made up of four people — one rabbi of Hassidic, one of Reform, and one of Conservative lineage, and a feminist theologian. In 1996, the United Nations named him one of the forty "Wisdom Keepers" from around the world, for a gathering connected with Habitat II.

Waskow received a Ph.D. in United States history from the University of Wisconsin in 1963. Through the 1960s, as a Fellow of the Institute for Policy Studies, he joined scholarly writing on race relations, military strategy, and conflict theory with leadership in the struggle to end the Vietnam War. With his brother Howard he is co-author of *Becoming Brothers* (Free Press, 1993), a "wrestle in two voices" about the struggles and reconciliations between them. He has taught at Swarthmore College, Temple University, and the Reconstructionist Rabbinical College. He has led a number of such inter-religious groups as the International Coordinating Committee on Religion and the Earth, and in 1996 held the Gamaliel Chair in Religion, Peace, and Justice created by the Lutheran community of Milwaukee.

He first learned story-telling at the knee of his grandfather "Pop" Waskow, and has been much encouraged by the work of Penninah Schram to foster the renewal of Jewish story-telling.

The two Oceans inserted that name into their individual names when they were married in 1986. Both were members of the editorial committee that created *Or Chadash (New Light)*, the innovative guide to Shabbat-morning prayer and celebration that was published by the P'nai Or Religious Fellowship. Together they have often led services drawing on *Or Chadash* for synagogues, havurot, institutes, and retreat centers throughout North America.

Together and separately, they have taught courses in various aspects of Torah at many National Havurah Institutes and P'nai Or/ ALEPH kallot. They have also done concerts of Jewish story-telling for the 92d Street "Y" in New York, for many synagogues and Hillel Houses, and for various other gatherings.

Between them they have four grown children, one son-in-law, and one daughter-in-law. They live in a lively integrated Philadelphia neighborhood, Mount Airy, among trees, streams, and a Toonerville Trolley, amidst an extraordinary community committed to Jewish renewal.